grk

AND THE
PHONEY
MACARONI

Other books by Josh Lacey

The Island of Thieves
The Sultan's Tigers
The Dragonsitter
A Dog Called Grk
Grk and the Pelotti Gang
Grk and the Hot Dog Trail
Grk: Operation Tortoise
Grk Smells a Rat
Grk Takes Revenge
Grk Down Under

grk

AND THE PHONEY MACARONI

Josh Lacey

Andersen Press · London

First published in 2012 by
Andersen Press Limited
20 Vauxhall Bridge Road
London SW1V 2SA
www.andersenpress.co.uk

This edition published in 2013

British Library Cataloguing in Publication Data available.

ISBN 978 1 84939 741 4

Printed and bound by CPI Group (UK) Ltd, Croydon, CR0 4YY

Chapter One

The dinosaur didn't move.

It hadn't moved for a hundred and fifty million years.

For most of that time it had been buried underground, but now it was standing in the main entrance hall of the Natural History Museum, staring at visitors through its empty eye holes.

Timothy Malt stared back.

Imagine being a dinosaur, he thought. How would that feel?

Actually, you wouldn't be able to feel very much at all. If you were dead. And had been for a hundred and fifty million years.

But imagine being a real dinosaur, thought Tim. A living, breathing dinosaur, knocking over trees and shaking the earth with every step. Would you realise that you were the biggest, meanest creature on the planet? Or would you go around feeling a bit nervous, always worrying that you were just about to bump into someone even bigger and meaner than yourself?

'Ah, there you are!' said a loud voice.

Tim turned round to see his mother marching across the museum's shiny floor to meet him. 'I've been looking for you everywhere. I thought we said we'd meet by the diplodocus.'

'This is the diplodocus,' said Tim.

'Is it?' Mrs Malt stared suspiciously at the dinosaur as if she suspected it of trying to trick her in some way. Then she looked around the hall. 'Where are Max and Natascha?'

'They're outside,' Tim told her. 'Max said he needed some fresh air and Natascha went with him. I told them I'd stay here and wait for you.'

That wasn't actually what Max had said. In fact, he'd said that museums were boring and if he had to look at one more stuffed bear or another lump of meteorite, he'd go completely nuts. But Tim couldn't see any reason to repeat that. He knew his mum wouldn't want to hear it. She'd immediately start complaining that she'd made such an effort to bring them all the way to the museum and didn't anyone appreciate all the work that she did on their behalf and no one understood how difficult it is to be a mother these days and how about saying 'thank you' for once rather than complaining all the time. Tim had already heard the same speech a million times from his mum and he really didn't want to hear it again, so he thought it was better just to say Max and Natascha wanted some fresh air.

It was half term and Mrs Malt had taken the day off work. This afternoon, she had brought the three children to the Natural History Museum and let them wander about all by themselves, looking at the exhibits. While they were seeing the museum, she sat in the café, checking her emails on her phone and catching up on some work. For Mrs Malt, that was the greatest miracle of modern technology: you could work even when you weren't working.

'Shall we go and find Grk?' said Tim. 'He must be going crazy.'

'Grk will be fine,' replied Mrs Malt. 'He doesn't mind spending a little time alone.'

'A little time? He's been there for hours!'

'He's been there less than an hour, actually,' said Mrs Malt. 'And the window is open, so he'll be absolutely fine. But you don't have to worry, we'll go and get him right away. Now, where are the others?'

'This way,' said Tim.

He and his mother walked out of the museum.

Just outside the main entrance Natascha Raffifi was sitting on a bench, scribbling in her journal. No one knew what she was writing. It might have been a diary or a novel or some poetry. She was very secretive about her writing. She never let anyone read her journal, and promised to inflict horrible punishments on anyone she caught sneaking a peek at the pages.

Max Raffifi was standing a little distance away, juggling with three stones that he'd picked up from the path. He noticed Tim and Mrs Malt walking towards him but he didn't acknowledge them. He didn't want to break his concentration.

As you probably know, Max and Natascha Raffifi were originally from Stanislavia, a small country in eastern Europe, not far from Russia. When their parents were murdered, they and their dog Grk came to live with the Malts. If you want to find out the full story you should read *A Dog Called Grk*.

'That's brilliant!' said Mrs Malt, clapping her hands.

3

'You've been practising, haven't you?'

'A bit.' Max didn't take his eyes from the stones.

In fact, he'd been juggling for several hours every day. Last weekend he'd twisted his ankle playing tennis, and the doctor had told him not to pick up a racket for at least the next fortnight. Nor was he allowed to run anywhere. Without tennis or jogging to keep him occupied Max had been going crazy. Until he discovered a set of three juggling balls that Tim had been given for Christmas and never opened.

'Let's go back to the car,' said Mrs Malt. 'We'll take Grk for a quick walk in the park. And then we'll be home in time for tea.'

Natascha closed her journal. She, Tim and Mrs Malt walked down the curving pathway that led to the exit on Cromwell Road. Max followed a few paces behind them, trying to juggle while he walked. He managed to keep it going for a few paces then he missed one of the stones, made a wild grab for it and ended up dropping all three on the ground. He left them there. Back in the car, he had his juggling balls, which worked much better than stones.

The four of them waited till the traffic lights turned red then crossed Exhibition Road and walked through a small, leafy square where Mrs Malt had parked on a meter.

There were two men standing beside the car. They appeared to be looking through the back window.

'Oh dear,' said Mrs Malt. 'I hope they're not traffic wardens.'

'They don't look like traffic wardens,' said Natascha.

She was right. Traffic wardens usually wear smart uniforms covered with shiny little buttons. These two strangers looked more like ordinary businessmen; they were wearing black suits and white shirts.

'What time is it?' Mrs Malt glanced at her watch. 'Even if they are traffic wardens, the ticket shouldn't have run out yet.'

She quickened her pace.

Tim, Natascha and Max hurried after her.

As Tim came closer to the two men he noticed something odd about them. Not their clothes. Or their shoes. Or their haircuts. All of which looked entirely ordinary. No, it was their faces which were odd: both men looked exactly the same. They must have been twins.

One of the men looked up and saw the Malts and the Raffifis walking towards him. He muttered to his companion. They stood there for a moment, deciding what to do, then turned and walked briskly in the opposite direction.

By the time that Tim, Natascha, Max and Mrs Malt had reached the car, the men had disappeared round the corner.

Inside the car Grk was standing on the back seat, wagging his tail, overjoyed to see them all. He threw himself at the window, his paws scrabbling against the glass, and barked desperately, begging to be let out.

'We're back!' called Natascha, waving through the window.

Tim said, 'Will you open the door, Mum? He must be suffocating in there.'

While Mrs Malt was opening the car, Max walked down to the end of the street and looked for the two men, but they seemed to have disappeared. He frowned. Who were they? Why were they looking in the car? Had they been planning to break in? But why would anyone be silly enough to break the window of a car that had a dog inside?

'Hey, Max! Come on!'

Tim beckoned. Grk was already out of the car, the lead clipped to his collar. The others were ready to go.

Max took one final look up and down the street but couldn't see any sign of the two men. He walked over to the others and they headed towards the park. Grk led the way, his tail wagging and his nose in the air.

None of them looked back the way that they had come.

Which was why none of them noticed two men about fifty metres behind them, darting from car to car and corner to corner, keeping out of sight while following them to the park.

Chapter Two

Earlier that day, not very far away, a small man had been speaking in a loud voice.

'Our country needs a new prime minister,' he said.

He might have been small, but he spoke with great authority.

'Our new prime minister must be strong,' he continued. 'He must be determined. And, more than anything, he must have courage. My friends, there is only one man in Italy who is fit to be our new prime minister, and this man is...Me!'

Giovanni Mascarpone, the thirteenth Duke of Macaroni, paused for a moment, waiting for the inevitable applause.

None came.

No one clapped. No one shouted. No one cheered. In fact, no one made any noise at all.

That was because no one could hear him.

The Duke of Macaroni was talking to himself.

He was standing in a lift, heading towards the top floor of one of the smartest hotels in London. While he was speaking, he had been looking at his own reflection in the mirror on the wall.

He liked what he saw.

The Duke of Macaroni was extremely short, but you only noticed that when you saw him standing next to someone else. When he was alone – in a photograph, for instance, or on TV – your eyes were immediately drawn to his handsome face. He had a strong chin, gleaming white teeth and a mane of thick, black hair. He was wearing a neatly tailored black suit, a white silk shirt and a blue tie. If you walked past him in the street, you would know immediately that you were looking at someone important, someone famous, someone who mattered.

He had been practising this speech again and again for the past few days, taking advantage of every spare moment to go over his words.

Tomorrow he would be back in Rome, standing in front of a thousand people, giving the most important speech of his life, and he didn't want to make any mistakes.

Cameras would broadcast his speech all around the country. Millions of Italians would hear his words. Millions of Italians would nod their heads. Millions of Italians would stamp their feet. Millions of Italians would wave their fists. Millions of Italians would join his party and vote for him.

That was his plan, anyway.

And that was why his speech needed to be perfect.

The lift pinged. The doors slid open. The Duke of Macaroni stepped out and walked briskly down the corridor towards the penthouse.

His bodyguards saw him coming and stepped aside.

The duke always posted two bodyguards outside his suite. He didn't like taking any risks. In this hotel, the security was impeccable, but it was always better to be safe than sorry.

Inside the penthouse, the duke found Maria, his wife's maid, and Peppi, his wife's little black and white dog, but there was no sign of Carla herself.

'Where is my wife?' he asked the maid.

'The duchess is getting ready, Your Excellency,' replied Maria. 'She just has to—'

'Getting ready?' interrupted the duke. 'But we're meeting some of the most important people in Great Britain. We can't be late! Where is she?'

'In the bathroom, sir. But she doesn't want to be disturbed.'

The Duke of Macaroni didn't care. He marched across the heavy carpet and rattled the bathroom door.

It was locked.

He hammered his fist on the door and shouted, 'Carla?'

There was no answer.

The duke shouted louder and hammered harder. 'Carla! What are you doing in there?'

His wife called back: 'I'll be out in a minute!'

'A minute isn't good enough! Come out now!'

'I can't.'

'Why not?'

'Because I'm not ready yet.'

'We're late,' shouted the duke through the wooden door. 'Can you hurry up?!'

'Relax, sweetie-poppet,' Carla shouted back. 'I told you already, I'll be out in a minute.'

The duke fumed.

Sweetie-poppet? Sweetie-poppet? What did she mean, sweetie-poppet?

Sometimes the duke was very glad that no one could hear his wife talking to him. At other times he wondered why he had ever married her. Yes, of course, she was one of the most beautiful women in the world, and he loved her, and, even more importantly, so did the Italian public. Even if they didn't want to vote for him as prime minister, they would vote for her to be the prime minister's wife. But why did she have to call him sweetie-poppet? And, even worse, why was she always so late?

The duke was Italian, so he was used to people being late, but his wife was later than anyone he had ever met. She was late for everything! Even the most important appointments. Didn't she understand that they were meeting some of the most powerful men and women in Great Britain? Didn't she care about her husband's ambitions? Didn't she want him to become Prime Minister of Italy? Didn't she want to be the prime minister's wife?

The Duke of Macaroni stomped back into the sitting room.

Maria had gone. She must be fussing around in her mistress's bedroom. But Peppi was there. And, as usual, as soon as Peppi saw the duke, he started growling.

Grrrr!

'Oh, shut up,' snapped the duke.

That was a mistake. At least Peppi thought so. He leapt down from the sofa and growled even louder.

Grrrrrrrrrr!

'Don't you dare growl at me!' yelled the duke.

Peppi growled again, baring his teeth.

Grrrrrrrrrrrrrrrrrrr!

The Duke of Macaroni wasn't in the mood to be growled at. Especially not by his wife's stupid little mutt.

They had never liked one another. From the moment that they met the duke and Peppi had been competing for Carla's affections. Each of them wanted to have her entirely for himself.

Of course, neither of them had any choice. Carla wouldn't give up Peppi for anything in the world, and the Duke of Macaroni wasn't going to change his choice of wife just because she had a dumb little dog, so the two of them had to put up with one another. In front of her, they even pretended to like one another. But when she wasn't looking, they showed their real feelings. Peppi bit the duke whenever he got the chance and the duke kicked Peppi as often as he could.

Like now, for instance.

No one was watching. Carla was in the bathroom and Maria was in the bedroom. It was the perfect opportunity for a little kick. The duke was wearing a pair of pointed, polished, black brogues, and he aimed one of them at the mutt, kicking him squarely in the ribs.

Peppi rolled across the carpet, waving his little legs in the air and squealing in agony.

The duke grinned. He felt better already. One little kick wiped away all his troubles. He had forgotten his wife and her infuriating lateness. He had even forgotten that the Prime Minister of Great Britain would be waiting in 10 Downing Street, wondering why the future Prime Minister of Italy was keeping him waiting.

I should kick Peppi more often, he thought to himself.

He got his chance right away.

Peppi picked himself up and threw himself across the room, determined to get his revenge on his mistress's husband.

Peppi's mouth was open. His teeth were barred. He nipped at the duke's ankle.

'Ow!' squeaked the duke.

If Peppi was human, he would have laughed. Instead he cheerfully waggled his tail and came back for another bite.

The duke tried to kick him.

Peppi dodged out of the way, then lunged back.

'Get off!' snapped the duke and tried to kick him again.

Peppi was too quick. He nipped the duke's other ankle.

Now the Duke of Macaroni was dancing around the room, trying to get out of the way. He jumped backwards. Then sideways. And lifted his leg out of harm's reach.

Peppi darted after him.

The duke swung around and gave the dog a vicious kick in its middle.

The tip of the duke's boot struck Peppi right in the ribs, lifting him off the ground.

The little black and white dog soared through the air and slammed headfirst into the middle of the marble fireplace.

Chapter Three

The Duke of Macaroni was panting.

He took a moment to get his breath back. Dancing around like this, moving his feet, trying to get away from a mad dog – it was tiring. He wasn't as fit as he used to be.

He told himself that he'd have to go back to the gym and hire a new trainer. If he wanted to be prime minister, he would have to be fit enough for anything. Walking up red carpets. Shaking hands with voters. Kissing babies. All of that took energy. Tomorrow morning, he told himself, he would go to his private gym and start a new exercise regime.

'Come on,' he snapped at the dog sprawled in the fireplace. 'What's wrong with you, Peppi? Are you scared? Don't you want to come and fight me again?'

The dog didn't move.

Peppi just lay there, his four feet spread out in different directions, his tail flopped on the carpet. He wasn't panting like the duke. In fact, his lungs didn't seem to be moving at all. Nor was any other part of his body. From his nose to his tail, Peppi was entirely still.

The duke stamped his foot on the floor, trying to elicit a reaction from the dog. 'Come on!' he hissed. 'Get up! Fight back! What kind of coward are you?'

Peppi didn't move.

He didn't even blink.

The smile slowly faded from the duke's face.

No, he thought.

It's not possible.

Is it?

He had just given the dog a little kick. Nothing too terrible. Nothing that he hadn't done a hundred times before.

He couldn't have...

Could he?

He threw himself to the ground, placed his hand on the dog's neck and checked his pulse.

Nothing.

No heartbeat.

The dog's body was still warm, but he wasn't breathing.

Peppi was dead.

The duke panicked.

He knew how much his wife loved that dog. Yes, of course, she loved him too, but he often thought that she loved her dog even more. If she was forced to choose between the two of them, she would probably choose Peppi.

What would Carla do when she discovered that the dog was dead?

And that her husband was responsible?

The duke knew the answer to that already.

She would kill him herself.

Or, even worse, she would ask for a divorce.

Italy was a conservative country and the Duke of Macaroni belonged to a conservative party. His supporters didn't approve of divorce. They would be appalled. And they would never vote for him.

They loved dogs too. All Italians loved dogs. Would they vote for a man who killed his own wife's dog?

Never.

His career was over.

His ambitions lay in ruins.

He might as well cancel his speech now. There was no point trying to give it. No one would be voting for him. There was no point meeting the Prime Minster now or travelling back to Rome this afternoon. He might as well give up all thoughts of a career in politics.

Unless...

A gleam appeared in the duke's eyes.

He had a thought. The beginning of an idea. Maybe he could do something. Maybe he could rescue this situation. Maybe...

He scooped up the dog in his arms and hurried towards the door. Just before he got out of the penthouse, Maria emerged from her mistress's bedroom. She saw the dog in her master's arms.

'I'm taking Peppi for a walk,' said the duke. 'Tell my wife that I'll be back in a minute.'

'Yes, sir,' said Maria. She was surprised. The duke never usually took Peppi for a walk. In fact, the duke usually made no secret of the fact that he couldn't stand Peppi. On many different occasions Maria had heard him begging his wife to get rid of her dog. And once, a few months ago, she even caught the duke kicking the dog. She didn't mention it, of course. She pretended she hadn't seen anything. That's what you have to do when your boss is a man as powerful as the Duke of Macaroni.

She did exactly the same thing now: she smiled politely, kept her mouth closed and didn't ask any questions. Instead she simply stepped aside, let her master leave and closed the door after him.

Chapter Four

The duke walked out of the suite with Peppi in his arms. His two bodyguards were standing in the corridor. The duke hissed at them: 'Come with me! Quick!'

Their names were Alberto and Antonio Gorgonzola. They were twins and they had worked for the duke for many years.

Right now, they were just as surprised as Maria to see their boss holding Peppi. They knew how much their boss hated that little mutt. They had never even seen him pat the dog, let alone pick him up in his arms and carry him around. But they knew better than to ask any questions. They simply stepped away from their post and followed their boss.

At the end of the corridor, there was a room where the hotel kept clean laundry. Two maids were sorting through sheets and towels, and giggling about some private joke. When they saw the man standing in the doorway, they both went quiet. They didn't know who he was, but they could tell from his suit and his manner that he was a guest at the hotel. Probably a very rich and important guest. One who must be obeyed. He spoke English with a strong Italian accent. 'I need this room. Leave us alone, please, for fifteen minutes.'

'Yes, sir,' said one of the maids. She nodded at her companion. They put their sheets on the shelves and filed silently out of the room, trying not to look at the man or the dog in his arms.

When the maids had gone, the Duke of Macaroni ordered one of his bodyguards to close the door. Then he showed them what he was holding in his arms. 'You know what this is?'

Alberto and Antonio had both worked for the duke for several years and they knew him well. He wasn't the type of man who made jokes. Nor was he the type of man who liked other people to make jokes. So, right now, neither of them was quite sure what to say.

'Come on, come on,' insisted the duke. 'You're not idiots. What is this?'

'A dog, boss?' suggested Antonio.

'Yes, but which dog?'

'Peppi?' suggested Alberto.

'Exactly! It's Peppi. Well, it *was* Peppi. Now, it's just a dead dog. Actually, it's a dead dog who is causing me a lot of problems. Now, Alberto, Antonio, I need you to help me. I need you to get rid of this dead dog. Can you do that?'

'No problem,' said Antonio.

'Consider it done,' said Alberto.

'Thank you.' The Duke of Macaroni thrust the dead dog at the nearest of the two bodyguards, who happened to be Antonio. 'And when you've got rid of Peppi, you have to find him again. Do you understand?'

For a moment neither of them answered him.

Then Antonio said, 'I thought you wanted us to get rid of him.'

'I do.'

'Then why do you want us to find him again?' asked Alberto.

'I don't want you to find Peppi,' said the duke. 'I want you to find another dog which looks exactly like Peppi. I want to replace this Peppi – the dead one – with another Peppi. A living one. But he has to look exactly like Peppi so my wife won't know the difference. Can you do that?'

'I dunno, boss,' said Antonio.

The duke gritted his teeth. 'What do you mean, you don't know?'

'I mean... I mean...'

'Yes?'

'I mean, yes, boss. No problem, boss. We'll do it right away.'

'Good.'

'But, um, boss, where are we going to find a dog which looks exactly like Peppi?'

'I don't know,' snarled the Duke of Macaroni. 'And I don't care. But you'd better do it quickly. Right now I'm going to meet the prime minister with my wife. I'm going to tell her that you've taken Peppi for a walk. We've got meetings all day. As soon as they're over we'll drive to the airport and get on my plane and fly home to Italy. When we get on that plane I want to find you waiting for us. With Peppi. The new Peppi. The living, breathing Peppi. Do you understand me?'

'Yes, boss,' said Antonio and Alberto at the same time.

'Good.'

Without another word the Duke of Macaroni turned on his heel, marched smartly out of the laundry room and closed the door after him, leaving his two bodyguards with a lot of clean sheets, even more clean pillowcases and one dead dog.

Chapter Five

Antonio Gorgonzola looked at his twin brother and said, 'What are we gonna do?'

'What do you mean, what are we gonna do?' replied Alberto.

'I mean, what are we gonna do?'

'You heard the boss. We're gonna get rid of this dog and find another, just like he said.'

'Getting rid of this dog, that's no problem. But where are we going to find another?'

'That's a good question.' Alberto scratched his head. 'I dunno. Where do you get a dog?'

'How about a dog shop?'

'Where are we going to find a dog shop?'

'This is a big city. There are shops selling everything here. Some of them must sell dogs.'

'Then let's go find one.'

Alberto wrapped the dead dog in a pillow case. Antonio stepped out of the laundry room and looked both ways, checking that the duchess wasn't anywhere nearby. Meeting her now would ruin everything.

The corridor was empty. Antonio nodded to his brother and the two of them hurried towards the lift.

They took it all the way down to the basement. Like any good security men, they had already checked out all the hotel's facilities. They knew the locations of the entrances and exits. They had explored the gym, viewed the swimming pool and poked around the kitchen. They had also discovered that all the hotel's rubbish ended up in the basement, packed into twenty enormous bins which were emptied every evening, and that was where they went now.

Just before Antonio tipped the pillowcase into the nearest bin Alberto cried, 'Wait!'

'Why?' asked Antonio.

'His collar.'

'What about it?'

'Take it off.'

'Why?'

'Because we're gonna put it on the new Peppi, right? So the duchess don't know the difference.'

'Oh, yeah.' Antonio reached into the pillowcase, removed Peppi's collar and stuffed it into his pocket, then tipped the dead dog into the bin.

'Rest in peace,' said Alberto.

'Amen,' added Antonio.

Next they went to a pet shop and asked to buy a dog.

'What kind of dog?' asked the man behind the counter.

Antonio and Alberto didn't have a picture of Peppi, and their English wasn't good enough to describe him very well, so they simply asked to see every dog in the shop.

Not one of them looked like Peppi.

'Why don't she have a poodle like anyone else?' asked Alberto.

'You know the story,' said Antonio. 'She found Peppi in the road, that's why she loves him. It's cute, huh?'

'Cute? You think this is cute? Us getting mashed by the duke because we can't find a dog – that's cute?'

'No, no, that's not cute. But the dog, he's cute.'

'He *was* cute,' corrected Alberto. 'Now he's nothing.'

They stood for a moment, remembering Peppi, and then they remembered something even more important: if they didn't find another dog very soon – a dog which looked exactly like Peppi – they would probably be turned into dog food themselves.

Alberto turned to the owner of the pet shop and asked if there was anywhere else in London where you could buy a dog.

Since then, the Gorgonzola brothers had been to Battersea Dogs & Cats Home, the Wandsworth Refuge for Abused Pets, the Kensal Green Canine Sanctuary and six more pet shops. They had seen dogs of all breeds and colours and shapes and sizes. A few of these dogs looked a little like Peppi. One had a nose just like his. Another had the right type of tail. A third had the perfect legs, and a fourth had a body which might have belonged to Peppi himself. If Antonio and Alberto could have mashed all those dogs together, they would have had another Peppi right here and right now. Unfortunately they weren't dog-surgeons or dog-scientists, and they didn't have time to find one.

In fact, they didn't have time for anything. Any minute now the duke and duchess would be heading back to Heathrow Airport, where their private jet would be waiting to whisk them home to Italy.

Antonio and Alberto walked slowly and unhappily through the streets near their hotel, discussing what to do.

'Brazil,' said Antonio suddenly.

'Brazil?' Alberto repeated. 'What about Brazil?'

'I've heard it's nice.'

'So what if it's nice?'

'We could go there. And hide.'

'Even in Brazil, he'd find us.'

Antonio didn't argue. He knew his brother was right. Wherever they went, the Duke of Macaroni would find them. There was no point trying to escape to Brazil or anywhere else. They might as well just give themselves up and wait for their punishment.

Alberto looked at the display on his phone. 'He's gonna be waiting for us.'

'I know, I know.'

'He's gonna be furious.'

'I know, I know.'

'He's gonna kill us.'

'I know, I know.'

'So what are we going to say?'

'Maybe we could say...' Antonio thought for a moment, considering the different possibilities, then shook his head. 'I dunno, Alberto. We can't say nothing. We can't do nothing. We better just hope, whatever he does, it ain't too painful.'

'That's what I'm hoping too,' said Alberto.

Over the years Antonio and Alberto had done many terrible deeds for the Duke of Macaroni. They had seen his anger and they knew how he treated anyone who annoyed him. Now, they knew, it would be their own turn to feel his fury.

'I don't believe it,' Alberto said suddenly.

'You'd better believe it,' his brother said. 'Because it's happening.'

'No, no. I'm not talking about us. I'm talking about that.'

They were walking alongside a row of parked cars. Alberto was pointing through the back window of the nearest.

Antonio stepped over to see what his brother was pointing at.

For a moment Antonio blinked, unable to believe what he could see.

Inside the car there was a little dog lying on the back seat.

The dog had white fur covered with black patches.

Just like Peppi's.

He had perky little ears and a tiny tail.

Just like Peppi's.

Now, seeing the two men peering at him, he jumped to his feet and barked at them.

He even sounded exactly like Peppi!

'He's perfect!' whispered Antonio.

Chapter Six

Tim, Natascha, Max, Mrs Malt and Grk walked through Hyde Park, breathing in the fresh air and searching for squirrels.

Well, that's not quite true. The four humans had very little interest in small furry rodents. But for Grk, not much could have been nicer than chasing a squirrel.

Of course, Grk had other pleasures in life too. Eating steak, for instance. Or biscuits. Or cheese. Or almost anything else. In fact, right now, here in the park, he would have very been happy to chomp on a juicy lamb chop or a tasty slice of bacon or a thick slab of steak, but there wasn't anything like that to be seen, so he concentrated all his attention on an equally delectable pleasure: chasing squirrels. He roamed across the grass, his nose in the air, his ears perked up, his eyes searching the trees and the bushes, searching for any sign of a squirrel.

What was that?

Over there! On the grass! What was it?

A pair of little grey eyes. A fluffy grey tail. Two tiny paws clamped around an acorn.

A squirrel!

Without a moment's hesitation Grk was off, tearing across the grass, head down, ears flattened, paws thumping on the ground, trying to reach the squirrel before it noticed him.

But the squirrel was ready for him. Like every other squirrel in the park, she knew all about the dangers of dogs. As soon as she caught a glimpse of a white shape streaking across the grass towards her she dropped her acorn and sprinted in the opposite direction, heading for the nearest tree.

The dog and the squirrel raced across the grass.

The humans weren't watching what happened. They'd all seen Grk chase hundreds of squirrels before and they knew he never caught them. Squirrels were just too fast for him. They always managed to find a tree and climb into the branches before he got near to them.

Suddenly they heard a dog barking.

It wasn't a happy bark.

It was a desperate bark.

A bark which said: *Help me!*.

Tim, Natascha, Max and Mrs Malt looked around, searching for the source of the bark.

There was no sign of the squirrel. She must have disappeared into a tree and would now be hiding in the branches, screeching and chattering, warning other squirrels within earshot that there was a dog on the loose.

But they could see Grk.

There he was!

In the arms of a large man wearing a white shirt and a black suit.

It was one of the men who had been staring at Grk through the window of the car. His twin was standing nearby. As Tim, Natascha, Max and Mrs Malt watched in horror, the man reached into his pocket, pulled out a black bag and thrust it over Grk's head.

The bag completely covered the little dog, trapping him, wrapping him up and preventing him from seeing where he was or what might be happening. Grk kicked and scratched and yapped and snapped, but he couldn't get himself out of the bag.

'Grk!' yelled Natascha.

Hearing her voice, Grk struggled even more desperately, trying to push himself out of the black bag, but the man was too strong for him. Tucking the bag firmly under his arm, he turned and ran in the opposite direction, followed by his companion.

Max started running.

Tim went after him.

Natascha screamed again, even louder: 'Stop! Thief!'

Mrs Malt yelled out to other people in the park: 'Someone, help! Please, can't someone help us!'

But no one took any notice. The park was full of people, but all of them were walking their dogs or talking on their phones or chatting to their friends, and they didn't want to get involved in someone else's problems.

Max was a fast runner. He usually jogged at least three miles a day. But he'd sprained his ankle and every step sent a jolt of agony burning through his body.

The doctor had told him not to run for a month in case he caused permanent damage, but Max didn't care about that now. He had more important things to do. Compared to Grk's safety, damaging his leg didn't matter at all. He sprinted across the grass.

Tim wasn't far behind.

By the time the dognappers reached the edge of the park, Max had almost caught up with them.

They were bigger than him, but he didn't even pause to worry about that. He reached out, his arm at full stretch, and grabbed the black bundle that enclosed Grk.

He couldn't get a good grip.

He was just lunging forward, trying to wrap his fingers more securely around the bag, when the big man swung round and punched Max in the face.

Max staggered backwards. He raised his hands to protect himself, but he wasn't quick enough. The man punched him again, knocking him to the ground. Then the other twin was there too. Together, both of them lashed out, kicking Max with their pointed shoes.

By the time Tim reached Max, the men had gone.

Max was sitting up, tenderly touching his face, as if he was trying to work out how many bones had been broken and how many teeth had been knocked out.

'Are you all right?' Tim asked. 'Where does it hurt?'

Max could have said, 'Everywhere'. That would have been the truth. Instead he said, 'Go after them.'

'What about you? Don't you need help?'

'I'm fine. Just catch them. Go!'

Tim didn't waste any more time. He could see that the two men had run out of the park and were already halfway across the road. Another few seconds and they'd be gone for ever.

He started running.

Chapter Seven

Tim ran through the streets.

On either side of him, the buildings were tall and white. He didn't know where he was. He'd always lived in London, but it was a huge city and he was sure he'd never been down these particular streets before. That didn't matter. He didn't need to know where he was. He just needed to keep those two men in sight.

It wasn't easy. He'd been running a long way already and he was getting tired.

The two men were bigger than him, and fitter than him, and could run much faster than him, and ordinarily they would have outpaced him long ago. But one of the men was carrying a small dog who was wriggling and jiggling, biting and scratching, desperately trying to escape, and that slowed him down.

Even so, Tim fell further and further behind.

He wished he'd listened to Max.

Every day, Max went jogging and he always invited Tim to come too. Tim invariably said no. He had better things to do. Playing computer games, for instance. Or lying on the sofa, tickling Grk's ears.

I'm an idiot, thought Tim. I shouldn't have wasted all that time playing games and tickling Grk's ears. I should have put on my shorts and my shoes and gone jogging with him. If I was fit, then my legs wouldn't hurt so much, and I'd be able to breathe, and I wouldn't be falling further behind every second, losing sight of those two robbers.

By the time Tim reached the corner, the men were already running round the next corner, far ahead of him.

He put his head down and sprinted after them.

A car screeched to a halt in the middle of the road. The driver leaned out of his window and shook his fist, but Tim took no notice. Nor did he say sorry. He didn't have time to worry about stuff like that now. All that mattered was keeping up with Grk.

But he wasn't moving fast enough. By the time he reached the next corner, the robbers had gone.

He looked one way, then the other, desperately searching for any sign of two running men, but he couldn't see them. Nor did he know which way to go. They could be anywhere.

Then he saw them.

They weren't running any more. They were getting into a taxi.

And he could see Grk too, still snarling and biting and barking and struggling desperately to escape. He'd managed to wriggle his head out of the black bag, but the rest of his body was still trapped in that big man's arms, unable to get away.

The taxi door slammed shut. The men were inside, taking Grk with them. The cab drove away from the kerb and eased into the traffic.

Tim wanted to shout out – 'Stop! Stop that taxi! Stop those men! They've stolen my dog!' – but he knew he didn't have the energy to run and shout at the same time, and so decided just to run.

Straight down the middle of the road.

Cars swerved.

Horns beeped.

Drivers shouted.

Tim kept running, taking no notice of them. He didn't care who shouted at him. He wasn't interested in his own safety. He just had to catch up with that taxi and stop these men stealing Grk.

But he was falling further and further behind.

The taxi was moving faster now, turning another corner, getting away from him. Then it was gone.

A few seconds later Tim raced round the same corner and saw the taxi waiting at a red light. No: the light was changing. It was amber now. And green. The taxi moved forward.

Tim ran faster. His lungs hurt. His legs too. He'd never catch the taxi. He knew that. He was sure of it. He wasn't fast enough. But he didn't stop running. But he wasn't going to give up. Not yet. Not while he could still move. Not till his legs gave way under him.

Mrs Malt looked around, searching for her son. She couldn't see him. She turned to Max and asked, 'Where's Tim?'

'I don't know,' said Max mournfully. 'If I did, I'd be there too. It's my own stupid fault! I should have stopped them.'

'What are we going to do now?' asked Natascha.

'I don't know,' said Max again. He was sitting on the grass, clutching his nose. Blood seeped through his fingers and dribbled down his shirt. His face was drawn and his voice was despairing. He blamed himself for what had just happened. He was the oldest and the most responsible. He was the fastest too. If only he hadn't sprung forward like an idiot, letting himself get hit, he could have stopped those two men.

Natascha could see how her brother was feeling. She spoke to him softly in Stanislavian, telling him not to blame himself. He'd done his best, she said. And he needn't worry: they would find Grk. And Tim too. She didn't know how, or where, or even when, but she was quite sure that they would soon find both of them.

While Max and Natascha were talking in their own language, Mrs Malt reached into her handbag and pulled out her phone. She could have called her husband to tell him that their son had gone missing. Or she could have called the RSPCA to complain about the way that those two men had treated Grk. She could even have called the park authorities to report a pair of identical dogsnatchers.

But she didn't call any of them. Two men had punched a boy to the ground. Tim and Grk were both gone. This was too urgent for the park authorities, the RSPCA or even her husband.

She pressed the same key three times on her phone, dialling 999, then asked the operator to connect her directly to the police.

Chapter Eight

If you had been watching the news that day you wouldn't have seen any footage of a boy running out of Hyde Park and into the streets of South Kensington.

Nor would you have seen a pair of dogsnatchers in the back of a taxi.

But you would have seen the Duke of Macaroni arriving at 10 Downing Street and meeting the prime minister.

The two men turned to face the cameras, smiled and shook hands. Beside them, the Duchess of Macaroni and the prime minister's wife kissed one another on the cheek.

A hundred cameras filmed their handshake and broadcast the scene around the world. Sixty journalists shouted questions, some in English and others in Italian, but the duke and the prime minister took no notice. They smiled their practised smiles once more for the cameras, then turned and walked into 10 Downing Street, followed by their wives, their advisers, their speech-writers and their translators.

Inside the prime minister's home they chatted politely about the weather and exchanged gifts. On behalf of the British government, the prime minister handed over a large wooden crate filled with Earl Grey tea. For the prime minister, the duke had brought three boxes of peaches from his own trees on the Macaroni estates.

Once they had thanked one another for such delightful presents, they spent the rest of the morning discussing important matters like the future of the world and the price of olive oil.

At half past twelve the prime minster was called away. The duke and duchess had lunch with the Foreign Secretary, followed by coffee with the Chancellor, a walk in the garden with the Secretary of State for Rural Affairs and a cup of tea with representatives from the Council for British–Italian Friendship and Mutual Understanding.

In the afternoon they climbed into a large black Rolls Royce and headed to Heathrow Airport, where their private plane would be waiting to whisk them back home.

As soon as the duchess was sitting inside the car she said, 'Where's Peppi?'

'Peppi?' repeated the duke stupidly as if he'd never heard the name before.

'He's my dog, darling. I haven't seen him all day and he must be missing me. You know how he is when he doesn't see me for a whole day. Where is he?'

'I don't know.' The duke looked around the car as if he might be able to spot a small dog that his wife had overlooked. 'He doesn't appear to be here.'

'I can see that, darling. So where is he?'

'Maybe he's still walking with Antonio and Alberto.'

'My Peppi walks for an hour a day, not five hours! What have they done with him? Where is he?'

'Darling, I told you, I don't—'

'Where is he?' interrupted the duchess.

'Give me a moment and I'll find out.' The duke reached for his phone and rang Alberto. After a short conversation he switched off the phone and turned back to his wife. 'You don't have to worry, my dear. Peppi is meeting us at the airport.'

The duchess stared at her husband. 'At the airport?'

'That's right. He will be waiting for us on the plane.'

'On the plane? But why? He should have been here in the car!'

'Antonio and Alberto wanted to show him the sights of London. The tour took longer than expected so they're coming directly to the airport and meeting us on the plane.'

The duchess stared suspiciously at her husband. 'You'd better be telling the truth,' she said.

'Of course I'm telling the truth,' smiled the duke.

It was a smile that had charmed the hearts of millions of Italian voters, persuading them to put a cross against his name in the voting booth, but it didn't work with his wife. She said, 'My darling, do you know what I would do if anything ever happened to that dog?'

The duke laughed nervously. 'What could possibly happen to Peppi? He's as strong as an ox! He's going to live longer than either of us.'

'I hope so,' said Carla. 'But if anyone ever hurt him, you know what I would do, don't you?'

'I imagine, my darling, you would be angry.'

'I wouldn't be angry.'

'You wouldn't?'

'No,' said Carla. 'I would be furious. And, like any self-respecting Italian woman, I would have my revenge. Whatever they did to my Peppi, I would do back to them, a hundred times worse.'

'You'd be right to,' said the duke, in what he hoped was a soothing voice. 'Only a monster would hurt your dog.'

The duchess didn't reply. She knew her husband was up to something – she just knew it! – but she didn't know what. Well, she'd find out soon enough. And if he was lying to her... She could worry about that later. For now she just wanted to see her beloved dog as soon as possible. She flicked her long, black hair out of her eyes, flopped against the cushions and stared through the window at the streets of London zipping past.

The duke stared out of the other window, nervously clicking his fingers.

Both of them, for their own reasons, prayed that Peppi would be waiting for them at the airport.

Chapter Nine

Inside the taxi Antonio and Alberto were having some problems.

They were both hard men.

They were used to doing hard things.

Bad things too.

In fact, if you made a list of bad things, Antonio and Alberto would have done just about all of them.

Not just ordinary bad things like dropping litter in the street or borrowing a book from the library and forgetting to take it back (although Antonio and Alberto had done both of those, and more than once), but seriously bad things. Like kidnapping, for instance. And murder. And other appalling crimes that I'm not even going to tell you about. Almost from the day that they were born, twenty minutes apart, first Alberto, then Antonio, they had been wicked in almost every way that you could possibly imagine.

But neither of them had ever stolen a dog before.

And they were finding it very difficult.

Whatever they did, the dog just wouldn't keep still.

Even worse, he kept trying to bite them.

When he couldn't get near them with his teeth – when they were holding his head, for instance – he tried to scratch them with his claws. Even when they pinned him to the taxi's back seat, one of them holding the back half of his body and the other holding the front, the dog didn't give up. He hardly even paused for breath. He carried on wriggling and snarling and scratching and biting and barking, trying to fight himself free of these two big bad bullies.

'What are we going to do?' hissed Antonio.

'Hold him,' said Alberto.

'I'm trying to! He keeps biting me.'

'He keeps biting me too.'

'You know what I wanna do?'

'I can guess.'

'I wanna get my gun and put a bullet in his head.'

'That's what I was gonna guess.'

'Shall I do it?'

'Don't be an idiot! We've got to get this mutt to the duchess in perfect condition.'

'And then what?'

'What do you mean, then what?'

'What's she gonna do with a dog like this? Ain't he gonna bite her?'

'The duke didn't say nothing about none of that,' said Alberto. 'We've just gotta do like he said and get the dog to the duchess. He can worry about all the rest of it.'

The taxi driver hadn't particularly liked the look of these two men, but he'd still stopped for them. They had a dog, after all, and he liked anyone who liked dogs.

He thought they must be twins. They certainly looked exactly alike. But he didn't ask any impolite questions.

He simply stopped his taxi, listened to where they wanted to go, then waited for them to clamber into the back. And started driving.

As he drove he watched them in the mirror, and he didn't like what he saw.

They weren't treating their dog very well.

In fact, they were treating their dog extremely badly.

The driver was a dog lover himself. He and his wife had two pugs at home. They were called Piggles and Wiggles, and the best part of his day was parking his taxi outside his house, opening the front door, hurrying into the hall and tickling their tummies while they rolled around on the floor, wagging their tails and yapping with delight.

He didn't know anything about the two men in the back of his taxi. He didn't know who they might be or where they came from. But he could see that they were mistreating their dog and he didn't like that at all.

Finally he couldn't take it any more. He turned the wheel, swerved to the side of the road and stopped the taxi.

'That's Gloucester Road tube station,' he said, pointing out of the window. 'If you want to go to Heathrow, you can catch a train from here.'

Neither Antonio nor Alberto could speak very good English, so the driver had to repeat himself three times before they understood that he was asking them to get out of his taxi.

'Whatsa problem?' asked Alberto, his accent so strong that he could hardly even understand himself.

'There's no problem,' said the driver, who didn't like getting into arguments with customers. 'I'm afraid I just can't take you to Heathrow. If you want to get there, I suggest you go into that station and catch a train.'

'We wanna taxi,' said Antonio.

'Then you'd better find another,' said the driver. 'I'm not taking you any further.'

'But why not?' Antonio asked.

'Whatsa problem?' added Alberto.

The driver sighed. He could see that he was going to have to tell the truth. 'Your dog.'

'Whaddabout the dog?'

'He's the problem.'

'You're speaking right, my friend,' said Alberto. 'The dog, he is one big problem. Now, please, sir, you will drive us to the airport.'

'I've already told you,' said the driver. 'I can't.'

'You wanna money? You wanna more money?' Alberto pulled out a handful of twenty-pound notes and pressed them against the glass. 'Here! How mucha money you wanna?'

The driver glanced at the money and shook his head. He wouldn't usually earn that much in a whole day, but that didn't matter. Even if these two men had been offering him a whole week's wages, he wouldn't take anyone in his taxi who treated their dog so badly.

'I'm sorry,' he insisted. 'You've got to get out of my cab.'

Chapter Ten

Tim was exhausted. His legs ached. His lungs were burning. He felt as if he was about to be sick. But he didn't stop running. He wasn't going to stop till his heart stopped or his lungs exploded or his legs broke – or he caught up with Grk.

Then he saw the taxi pulling over to the side of the road and coming to a halt beside the tube station.

The two men got out of the taxi. One of them turned back to wave his fist and shout a few Italian insults at the driver. The other stepped into the road and waved his arms at another taxi. When it stopped he thrust a bundle of twenty-pound notes through the open window and yelled at the driver.

A moment later the two men were clambering into the second taxi. Grk was still struggling, but they were too strong for him. They thrust him onto the back seat and slammed the door.

While all this was happening Tim had come closer. He was almost level with the taxi when it started driving down the street. In despair he hurled himself forward, trying to grab the back of the taxi or slap his hands down on the window, but he was too late, too slow.

He knew he couldn't outrun this taxi. He might have caught up with one of them, but he didn't have the strength left in his muscles to catch another. So he ran across the street to the first taxi instead and rapped on the window.

The driver looked at him, surprised. 'Hello, son.'

Tim was so breathless that he could barely get the words out. 'They've stolen ... They've stolen ...'

'Stolen what?'

'My dog.'

'Who has?'

'Them!'

The driver looked in the direction that Tim was pointing. He understood immediately what was going on. Yes, it all made sense. He knew there was something dodgy about those two blokes.

'Get in,' he said.

Tim yanked open the door and tumbled onto the back seat.

Once Tim got his breath back he told Tony what had happened.

Tony – that was the driver's name. 'I was christened Anthony,' he said. 'But no one's ever called me that, except my mother, and she's been dead for twenty-three years, God rest her soul.'

'I'm Tim,' said Tim.

'Good to meet you, Tim. Now, tell me about these guys. Who are they? And why have they stolen your dog?'

'I wish I knew,' said Tim.

It was a good question. Why would anyone want to steal Grk?

He was a small, black and white dog who wasn't worth anything.

Not to anyone except Tim, Max and Natascha, anyway.

He didn't have an exclusive pedigree. Nor did he have an expensive heritage. He'd never won any dog shows, and he never would.

If you were planning to make money from a stolen dog, you wouldn't bother with a mutt like Grk. You'd try to grab a posh poodle, a debonair dachshund or an aristocratic Airedale.

So why had those two men stolen him?

Tim couldn't answer that, but he told Tony as much as he knew. He explained about the park and the squirrels, and the two men appearing and grabbing Grk and punching Max, and how he had chased them through the streets. 'But I don't know why they did it,' he said. 'Or who they are. I've never seen them before.'

'I think they're probably twins,' said Tony.

'I thought they must be too.'

'And they're definitely foreign.'

'How do you know?'

'Because they were in my cab. I heard them talking.'

'Oh, yes. Of course. So where are they from?'

'I don't know. I can't speak foreign. They might be from anywhere. But they're going home, I can tell you that much.'

'How do you know?'

'Because they wanted to go to Heathrow Airport. I suppose they could be staying in a hotel there or meeting

44

someone, but my guess is they're catching a plane.'

'Heathrow? But that's miles away.'

'It won't take long. Unless the traffic's bad, but it shouldn't be, not at this time of day.'

'There's a problem,' said Tim.

'Oh, yes? What's that?'

'I haven't got any money. I won't be able to pay you.'

'Forget it.'

'I'll give you my address. I'll get my mum to send you a cheque.'

'I said, forget it. This is a free ride. We're on the trail of dognappers. I couldn't charge you for that.'

'Are you sure?'

'Sure I'm sure,' said Tony. 'I've got dogs myself. Now, what about your mum?'

'What about her?'

'Does she know where you are?'

'No.'

'Won't she be worrying?'

'I suppose she will,' said Tim.

Up to now Tim had hardly given a thought to the others. He'd left them in the park without a backward glance and, since then, his mind had been fully occupied with thoughts of Grk and the thieves. But Tony was right: they'd be worried. In fact, they'd be panicking.

Mum and Dad would be, anyway.

Max and Natascha might not be. They knew Tim was able to look after himself. They'd trust him to get Grk back.

He just hoped he could.

'You should ring her,' said Tony.

'I don't have a phone.'

'Use mine. Do you know her number?'

'Yes, but—'

'No buts. Just ring her. Here you go.' Tony passed back a phone. 'She'll be worrying about you, Tim.'

'How do you know?'

'That's what mothers do. Go on, call her.'

Tim reluctantly punched his mother's number into the phone. He didn't want to speak to her, because he already knew what she'd say. First she'd tell him off for running away. Then she'd say that he wasn't old enough to go to Heathrow on his own, and chasing dognappers should be left to the police. Finally she'd order him to get out of the taxi right now this minute and wait for her to come and pick him up.

To Tim's relief his call went straight to answer phone. He left a message for his mum, explaining where he was and why. Then he handed the phone back to Tony and stared through the windscreen. By now they were driving fast on a six-lane highway, heading out of the city. Up ahead, separated from them by seven cars, he could see their quarry, the other taxi. Two heads were visible through the back window. Those were the two men, the two dognappers. There was no sign of Grk. He must be at their feet, pinned down, trapped, imprisoned, stuck in that black bag.

Hold on, thought Tim. We're just behind you. We're coming to get you. Don't worry, Grk. You'll be free soon.

He just hoped he was right.

Chapter Eleven

Every week more than a million travellers pass through Heathrow Airport

Almost all of them spend several hours in queues.

They queue to check in their baggage. They queue to show their passports. They queue to pass through security. They queue to buy magazines and cups of tea. They queue for the loo. They queue to take a place in the departure lounge. And finally they queue to board the plane.

There is only one way to avoid all these queues, and that's by having your own plane.

When Alberto and Antonio arrived at Heathrow Airport they didn't have to wait in any queues. They simply told their taxi to take them to a private gate at the back of the airport which most people didn't even know existed. They handed a large bundle of cash to the taxi driver and hurried inside, carrying a small, struggling dog between them.

They were so busy taking care of Grk, trying to stop him biting their hands or scratching their faces, that they didn't bother looking behind them, which was why they didn't see a small boy jumping out of his own taxi and running after them.

* * *

Tony sat in his taxi and stared at the gates hoping Tim was going to be safe.

When they'd arrived at the gate, Tim jumped out and ran after those two dogsnatchers without a moment's hesitation.

He must love that dog, thought Tony.

Tony wondered if he would do the same for Piggles and Wiggles.

Of course he would, he told himself. He'd do anything for them. If a pair of foreign dognappers tried to snatch *them* in the park he wouldn't rest till he'd found them and got his beloved pugs back again.

He wished he had two phones. He could have given one to Tim and kept the other for himself. Then he could have called the boy's mum and told her what was going on.

But he only had one phone and he'd given it away. He didn't like letting the boy go after those two creeps without a phone. While they were on the motorway, he'd given the phone back to Tim and told him to call the police if he got in trouble.

He realised now what he should have done. He should have taken the boy's mum's number. Then he could have found a payphone and called her and explained what was going on.

But he didn't know her number. He didn't even know her name. He couldn't contact her. He'd just have to hope the boy came back soon, bringing Tony's phone and his own dog.

* * *

48

Tim didn't know where he was going. He didn't know who he was chasing, either. Those two men might have been crooks or drug dealers or murderers. He knew nothing about them. But he didn't hesitate for a moment. Grk was in danger. Nothing else mattered. Never giving a thought to his own safety, he jogged through the airport, following the two men.

One of them was carrying Grk under his arm. The other was talking on a phone.

If Tim had shouted, they would have heard him. If he'd sprinted after them, he could have caught them. But he dropped back a few paces, knowing he couldn't stop them alone. If he confronted them they'd just knock him to the ground. He had to be clever and careful. He had to wait for the perfect moment to grab Grk back.

The two men stopped beside a door.

Tim hid behind a wall, watching them.

The two men seemed to be arguing. He wondered what they were saying.

They soon reached an agreement. One of them opened the door. They both stepped inside and the door swung shut behind them.

Tim darted out of his hiding place and ran across the road.

When he reached the door, he paused for a moment, listening, but he couldn't hear anything from the other side.

He opened the door and stepped through.

He found himself in a cool, quiet building. He could hear a distant humming noise as if several cars were warming up their engines. Ahead of him, he could see two more doors, a desk and one of the men who had stolen Grk.

Seeing Tim, the man smiled and said, '*Ciao*.'

Just as Tim was wondering where the other man had gone, a heavy object hit him on the back of the head and the world went black.

The Duke of Macaroni was furious. He paced up and down the aisle of his private plane, cursing and looking at his watch and staring out of the window and cursing some more. They should have left an hour ago. Back in Italy people would be waiting for him. He had a series of meetings lined up with his associates and advisers to discuss the speech that he would be giving tomorrow.

His speech! The most important speech of his life. The speech which would seal his bid to be prime minister of his beloved country. He needed to get home right now and practise what he was going to say.

He turned to his wife, who was sitting in a large armchair, sipping a cup of Earl Grey tea and reading this week's *Hello*, searching for pictures of herself.

'My darling,' said the duke. 'Why don't we just go home?'

'I'm not leaving without my Peppi.'

'You don't need to worry. Antonio and Alberto can bring him on another flight. You'll only be separated from him for a few hours.'

'You can go if you want to,' said the duchess. 'I'd rather wait for Peppi.'

'What about my speech?'

'You can give your speech without me.'

'No, I can't.'

'Why not, darling?'

'Because I can't! Of course I can't! What will people think if my wife is not standing beside me, watching me give the most important speech of my life?'

'Perhaps they will think she has stayed in London to look after her dog.'

'Oh, Carla! Don't you care about my campaign? Don't you want me to be prime minister?'

'Of course I do, darling,' said the duchess. 'But I can't leave without my Peppi. It's as simple as that.'

The duke shook his head. He couldn't believe it. Where were Alberto and Antonio? What were they doing? They just had to find a dog and bring him here. What could be so difficult about that? He turned his back on his wife and marched down the plane, searching for a private room where he could ring his men again without being overheard.

He closed the door, pulled out his phone and rang Alberto's number.

Antonio and Alberto looked down at the boy on the floor.

Then they looked at one another.

'What are we gonna do now?' asked Antonio.

'Gimme a minute,' said Alberto. 'I'll think of something.'

'Shall we kill him?'

'I don't know.'

'If you want me to kill him, I'll kill him.'

'I said I don't know.'

'If you don't want me to kill him, why don't we leave him here?'

Alberto shook his head. 'He's seen our faces. He'll be able to identify us. The duke won't like that.'

'Then let's kill him,' said Antonio. 'That way he can't identify nobody.'

Before Alberto could answer, his phone rang. He looked at the display. 'It's the duke,' he whispered, more to himself than to Antonio, and put the phone to his ear.

Immediately a volley of words came out the phone, telling him that they'd better get to the plane in the next five seconds – with a dog! – or the duke would murder both of them with his own bare hands.

'Don't worry,' said Alberto. 'We'll be there.'

A second volley of words shot from the phone.

'Yes, boss,' said Alberto. 'Right away, boss. See you there, boss.'

He switched off the phone, looked at Tim then at Antonio, and said, 'Pick him up.'

'Pick who up?'

'The boy.'

'Why?'

'Pick him up and I'll tell you.'

Chapter Twelve

The duchess looked at Peppi and wondered what was wrong with him.

She knew her dog very well. She probably knew him better than any other creature on the planet, including her husband, and perhaps even including herself. For many years he had been her constant companion and her closest friend.

Looking at him now, she could see that he was unhappy, but she didn't know why. She wondered how to help him.

He had just been brought onto the plane by those two thugs who worked for her husband and, for some strange reason, he didn't appear to be pleased to see her. If she and Peppi were separated he usually threw himself into her arms, wagging his tail and covering her face with little kisses. Today he squatted on the floor, his ears flattened against his skull, staring at her with an expression of intense suspicion.

'What's wrong, Peppi?' asked the duchess.

In reply, the dog growled softly.

The duchess was puzzled. Her dog had never growled at her before. Why was he doing it now? Was he cross with her? Was he upset that she'd abandoned him and forced him to spend the whole day with those two horrible thugs?

She crouched on the ground beside him and extended her hand to stroke his ears.

This time the dog growled more loudly and showed his teeth.

The duchess sprang backwards, suddenly worried that he might bite her.

But why would he want to bite her? He'd never bitten her before. What was wrong with him? Was he ill? Or depressed? Or had he been horribly mistreated by these two thugs?

While the duchess was asking herself these questions, the duke was beginning to panic. He cast angry glances at Antonio and Alberto.

Antonio and Alberto were panicking too. They tried to avoid the duke's eyes, looking everywhere around the cabin but at him.

The dog had passed its first test. It looked right. Even the duchess thought it was Peppi.

So why couldn't it pass its second test? Why couldn't it talk to her like a good little dog?

Couldn't it appreciate that its life had just improved beyond its wildest dreams?

Didn't it understand that it now belonged to one of the wealthiest women in the world? It'd never have to worry about anything ever again. It could just lie back and enjoy the life of a millionaire.

Given the choice, Antonio would have been more than happy to do that.

So would Alberto.

So why wouldn't this ungrateful little mutt?

* * *

Grk was feeling confused.

He was a small dog in a big world so he was used to confusion. Strange things were always happening to him and he usually couldn't understand why. But today had been much worse than usual.

First those crooks grabbed him and squeezed him and hurt him and wouldn't let him go. Then they forced him to ride in a couple of taxis. And now this strange woman kept wanting to stroke him. It was all so confusing!

And not just confusing.

Annoying too.

He wanted to get home. He wanted to see Tim and Natascha and Max. He wanted his own bowl and his own basket. More than anything he wanted to get out of this room and away from these four strange, unpleasant people. He didn't like the look of them, or the smell of them either. Those two thugs were the worst. He'd spent half the afternoon with his nose stuffed in one or other of their armpits, and he never wanted to do that again. He didn't know much about the other two, the small man and the tall woman, but he didn't want to discover any more. He just wanted to go home.

He looked around the room, searching for an escape route, but he couldn't see anywhere to go. The door was closed. So was the window. What could he do? Where could he go? How could he get away from all these horrible people and back to the ones that he loved?

* * *

The duchess fixed Antonio with a fierce stare. 'What have you done to my dog?' she said.

'N-n-no-nothing,' stammered Antonio.

'Nothing? Nothing? Then why is he like this?'

Antonio nervously shrugged his shoulders. 'I don't know.'

The duchess turned to the other twin. 'How about you? Did you do something to him?'

'Of course not,' said Alberto. 'He's been very happy all day.'

'Happy? You call this happy? Look at him!'

They all turned to stare at Peppi.

Grk stared angrily back.

'What's wrong, Peppi?' said the duchess.

In reply, Grk growled again.

The duchess shook her head. More to herself than anyone else, she murmured, 'I've never seen him so unhappy.' Then she turned to her husband. 'Do you know what's going on? Do you know what they've done?'

'I have no idea,' said the duke. 'Antonio, Alberto, please tell the truth. Have you done anything to Peppi?'

'No, boss,' said Antonio.

'Nothing,' said Alberto.

'You must have done something,' said the duchess. 'Why else would he be so miserable?'

'I don't know,' said Antonio.

'Me neither,' said Alberto.

'Did you feed him?' said the duchess.

'No,' said Antonio.

Which would have been a perfectly good answer except, at exactly the same moment, Alberto said, 'Yes'.

The duchess turned from one of them to the other. 'Which is it? Yes or no?'

This time Antonio said 'Yes' and Alberto said 'No'.

But the duchess didn't notice. She had seen something even worse. 'He's naked!' she cried.

Antonio and Alberto stared at her, wondering what on earth she could be talking about. Naked? This dog? Of course he was! When had he ever worn clothes?

'My beautiful Peppi,' sighed the duchess. 'What have they done to you? They've stripped you naked!' She turned to the two men. 'Where is it?'

'Where's what?' asked Antonio.

'His collar, you idiot! Where is his collar?'

'Oh! The collar! It's here.' Alberto reached into his pocket and pulled out Peppi's diamond-studded collar.

'Why did you take it off? Were you planning to steal it?'

'Of course not!'

'Then why did you take it off?'

'Because, erm, because of the, erm—'

'X-ray machines,' suggested Antonio.

'Yes, that's right, we had to take it off because the x-ray machine. They wouldn't let him through with the collar on.'

'It doesn't matter. Just hand it over. Thank you.' The duchess took the collar from Alberto and knelt down. 'Come here, Peppi. My poor baby, let's put your collar back on. No wonder you're so unhappy. Come on, baby, let me— Ow!'

The duchess sprang backwards, clutching one hand with the other.

She couldn't believe it.

Peppi had bitten her.

He had never done that before. Not even when he was sick with the flu.

The duchess wasn't angry. Not with Peppi, anyway. She knew that there was only one possible reason why he would bite her: he must be upset. These two idiots must have been mistreating him. She would deal with them later. She would think of an appropriate punishment and take great pleasure in administering it. But that could wait. For now she only cared about Peppi. She stood up, walked over to her handbag, reached inside and pulled out a little leather pouch.

Grk was a connoisseur of good smells.

With one little sniff he could distinguish between every brand of dog food on the market.

From the top of a house he could tell what someone was taking out of the fridge in the basement.

All the way across a park he could tell the difference between a discarded cheese sandwich in a bin and half-eaten kebab dumped on a bench.

But he'd never smelt anything like this.

It was extraordinary. It was amazing. It was exquisite.

Whatever it was, he wanted it.

He turned his head from side to side, searching for the source of the smell, and saw the duchess.

She was kneeling down again, looking at him. Her right hand was outstretched. In her palm, she was holding a little brown treat.

'Do you want a sweetie?' she said.

She was speaking Italian, so Grk couldn't understand her. To be honest, he probably wouldn't have understood her even if she had been speaking English. He wasn't much good with words. But that didn't matter. To a dog like Grk, smells speak louder than words, and this particular smell shouted out at him at the top of its voice.

When Carla had married the Duke of Macaroni she had ordered his chef to create the best dog snack on the planet.

After weeks of experimentation, the duke's chef came up with the perfect recipe; a magical mixture of steak, chicken livers and double cream. No dog could resist them.

Not even Grk.

He darted across the room and gobbled the snack out of her hand. Then he bit down.

The mesmerising tastes slid across his tongue and down his throat.

Hmmmmmmmmmm.

It might have smelt good, but it tasted even better.

And now the duchess was offering him another.

Chapter Thirteen

Tim woke up in darkness.

He didn't know where he was or what had happened to him.

His head hurt.

He tried to reach up and touch his forehead to check for damage but discovered he couldn't move his arms. They were tied behind his back.

His legs were tied together too.

And there was a bandage over his mouth, preventing him from screaming for help.

The bandage almost covered his nose too. If it slipped a little and blocked his nostrils he wouldn't be able to breathe.

Why was he tied up? How had he got here?

Who had done this to him?

And what was that noise?

All around him he could hear the kind of loud, low humming that might be made by a big engine or a piece of heavy machinery. He wondered if he was locked in the boot of a car. Perhaps the humming noise was amplified in some way by the space and sounded louder than it would normally.

He remembered the two men who had dognapped Grk. He still didn't know anything about them. Who they were, why they had stolen Grk, or what they wanted with him.

But Tim presumed they must be the people responsible for putting him in here, wherever he was.

They weren't just dognappers. They were kidnappers too.

When he realised how they must have caught him, he felt very stupid.

While one of the men stood by that desk, smiling at him, the other must have been hiding behind the door. Tim had made life very easy for them; they just had to knock him on the head with a truncheon or a baseball bat, and he'd have fallen to the floor.

No wonder his skull hurt so much.

He wanted to check for blood and bruising.

He wanted a glass of water and some paracetamol.

He wanted to get up and walk around, stretching his arms and legs, making the blood move through his veins again.

He knew he wasn't going to get any of the things that he wanted.

He wondered when they would come and get him. How long would they leave him here? Had they just dumped him in this dark, cold place? Would he ever get out? Or would he stay here, hungry and thirsty, desperate to pee, for hours, then days?

Had they left him to die here?

He shuffled his limbs around, tested the boundaries of his prison.

He couldn't move far.

In every direction his movement was blocked. He couldn't roll over. He couldn't shift forward or backwards. He couldn't even stretch his legs.

He was in a box. Barely bigger than himself.

Without any warning, the world tilted onto its side. Around him the noise grew louder. Then the world righted itself again and the noise changed once more.

He suddenly realised where he was.

In a plane.

That was why they'd been driving to Heathrow Airport in the taxi. They were kidnapping Grk in order to fly him out of the country.

But where were they taking him? And why?

Perhaps the plane was packed with dogs of all shapes and sizes, destined for a dog farm or a dog zoo or dog factory.

Tim remembered seeing the movie of *One Hundred and One Dalmatians*. Maybe these dognappers were planning to slice Grk's fur from his body and turn him into a coat.

No chance, thought Tim. Whoever you are, I won't let you do anything like that.

Then he realised that he wouldn't be able to stop them. Not like this, anyway. Blindfolded and tied up and stuffed in a box – he couldn't do anything.

He didn't know who had kidnapped him, or where they were taking him, and he had no way of finding out, but Tim was sure of one thing. He didn't have long to save himself. The journey couldn't last longer than a few hours, and might only be one or two. Then the plane would land and they would come to fetch him.

Once they got their hands on him, he would never be able to escape.

Right now, on the flight, he had his best chance of saving himself, and probably his only chance. He had to free himself and then be ready to escape as soon as the plane landed.

He rubbed his hands together, pulling and stretching, trying to free himself from the ropes, but they were tied too tightly.

Tim didn't stop.

He pulled and pushed.

Pushed and pulled.

Trying to stretch the ropes.

It was exhausting. And so slow. For a long time, he didn't feel as if he was making any progress at all. Then the rope began to give a little. He could ease his hands apart a few millimetres.

His throat was dry. All his muscles ached. The rope was digging into his wrists, cutting off the supply of blood from his hands, making his fingers feel numb. It would have been very easy to roll over, lie down and give up. But Tim forced himself to keep going, pushing and pulling and pulling and pushing, biting his lip to make himself forget the pain.

Chapter Fourteen

Mrs Malt was just about to call her husband and tell him what had happened when she noticed a tiny icon on her phone's screen, telling her that she had a message.

She had just spent ten minutes talking to the police, who had promised to send a car immediately, and another twenty minutes talking the Royal Parks Authority, who agreed to send a couple of wardens to assist the police. That had been half an hour ago, if not a lot longer, but no police cars had arrived yet. What was taking them so long? Had they just left a message to explain what was happening? Had they found Tim?

Pressing a button to play the message, she put the phone to her ear.

Not far away, Natascha was walking along the boundary of the park, peering through the railings, searching for any sign of Grk, hoping he might have escaped and somehow sneaked back here on his own. She would have liked to start searching for Grk herself, but Mrs Malt had made her promise not go out of sight, and Natascha wasn't the sort of girl who broke her promises.

Max was sitting on the grass nearby. He wanted to be searching too. He wanted to be running through the streets, chasing those two men. But he didn't know where to go, and even if he had, he really needed a bit more time to recover from the beating that they had given him.

'It's Tim,' said Mrs Malt suddenly.

'Where?' Max looked around the park.

'No, not here. On my phone. He's left a message.'

When they had all listened to the message, Mrs Malt dialled the number that Tim had left.

The number didn't even ring. It went straight to the answer phone of a man named Tony.

'Hello, Tony,' said Mrs Malt. 'I don't know who you are, but my son seems to have used your phone to call me. His name is Timothy Malt and I'm very worried about him. Could you ask him to call me, please? Or call me yourself. As soon as possible.'

She left her number and thanked Tony for his help, then switched off the phone and looked at Max and Natascha.

'What are we going to do now?' she said. 'How are we going to find Tim?'

Chapter Fifteen

In a small private airport just outside Rome a large crowd was waiting on the asphalt watching the dark skies.

They had been waiting for a couple of hours already and they were getting impatient. What had happened to the Duke of Macaroni? Why hadn't he arrived yet? Were they going to be here all night?

Italians are always late. That's part of their national character. Along with pizza, pasta and the Leaning Tower of Pisa, Italians are famous for their lateness. But the Duke of Macaroni was supposed to be different. He didn't spend hours eating spaghetti with clams and then snoozing in the sun. He was more efficient. More ruthless. More modern.

So where was he?

Whispers and rumours went around the crowd.

There were storms over the Alps, said someone. The duke's plane must have been diverted and sent to a different airport.

There are reports of a crash in the mountains, said another voice in the crowd.

Then more and more voices added their opinions. Perhaps the duke had been killed. Perhaps his campaign was over. Perhaps he would never be the next Prime Minister of Italy. Perhaps he was—

Then a cry went up and a hand pointed at the sky, silencing all the voices in the crowd.

Ecco! Ecco il Duca!

There! There's the duke!

Inside the plane the duchess cradled Peppi on her knees and whispered, 'Don't worry, my darling. I know how much you hate flying, but you'll be safe with me.'

Grk couldn't understand a word that she was saying, but that didn't matter to him. He was used to it. He only knew about three words, so he usually couldn't understand what people were saying to him. He wagged his tail anyway, hoping she would give him another of those delicious snacks.

At the other end of the private plane the duke was sitting in an armchair, talking to the Gorgonzola twins. During the flight they had finally had a chance to tell him everything that had happened in London, describing their hunt for a dog, their capture of Grk, and their unfortunate kidnapping of a small boy who was currently tied up in the cargo hold.

'We don't have any choice,' whispered the duke, not wishing to be overheard by his wife, the cabin crew or any of the advisers who had been sharing the flight. 'You'll have to find a way to get rid of him.'

'You mean kill him?' asked Antonio.

'Of course I do,' whispered the duke. 'But be careful. No one must ever find him. I don't want anyone to be able to connect him with me – or with that dog. Do you understand?'

'Yes, boss,' said Alberto.

Tim could feel the plane descending. He knew he didn't have long. They'd be landing soon.

He pulled off his blindfold. He still couldn't see anything. He was in darkness.

He pushed the roof. It didn't move.

He pushed the sides of the box. They didn't budge, either.

He untied the rope around his ankles. Now he was entirely free. He just had to get out of this box.

He lay down on his back, bent his legs and put his feet on the lid. Then he pushed. And pushed. Straining every muscle in his body.

Suddenly the plane bumped, throwing him forward. Then bumped again and slowed down. He could hear the engines screaming. They must be landing.

He bent his knees again and pushed his feet even harder against the top of the box.

He could feel the wooden lid straining.

He pushed harder.

Suddenly the lid popped open.

He sat up. Then stood up. And looked around.

He'd been right. He was in the cargo hold of a small aircraft. In the gloom he could just make out the shapes of bags and boxes and suitcases stacked against the walls. Down at the far end there was a door. It would be locked from the outside, he was sure of that. Even when they landed, he wouldn't be able to get out. So what could he do? He knew they'd be coming for him soon.

He pulled himself out of the wooden crate.

Strewn on the floor of the plane he saw twenty or thirty boxes. He picked one up. There was writing on the side. Squinting in the low light, he managed to make out the words FINEST EARL GREY TEA.

He could feel the plane tilting. They were heading for the ground. A few minutes from now, they would be landing. If he was going to save himself, he'd have to work fast.

He knelt down and gathered an armful of boxes.

The plane landed. The engines switched off. The door opened. And the crowd finally got what they were waiting for: a glimpse of the Duke of Macaroni. He stepped out of the plane, lifted his right arm and waved.

The crowd erupted in cheers and applause.

The duchess stepped out of the door and stood beside her husband, holding her little dog Peppi in both her arms.

The crowd cheered even louder and surged forward, trying to come closer to their beloved hero and his adoring wife.

Inside the plane, Antonio and Alberto talked in whispers. They had already agreed on a plan. They would take the boy away from here. They didn't want to leave any traces that could connect him to the duke. No blood, no hairs, nothing like that. They would take him to the woods on the other side of Rome. Once they were deep in the countryside, far from the nearest house, they would kill him. Then they would dig a hole and bury him. No one would ever find him. And no one would ever ask any awkward questions about the duchess's dog.

No one heard what they were saying. The three stewardesses had already left the plane, and so had the duke's six advisers. The pilot and copilot were in their cabin, writing a report on the flight from London. There was only one other person left in the plane, and he was locked in a box in the luggage compartment, tied up and blindfolded, and unable to move.

Alberto checked his gun, making sure it was loaded. Many years ago he had taken out his gun to shoot someone and pulled the trigger, only to discover that he'd forgotten to load it. That day he had been very lucky to survive, and he'd never made the same mistake again.

When he was sure that the gun was ready to fire he turned to Antonio. 'You ready?'

'I'm ready,' said Antonio, who had also checked his own gun.

'Then let's go.'

They walked down the plane together. At the door they called *'Ciao'* to the pilot and the copilot, who shouted *'Arrivederci'* back. Then they left the plane.

Antonio and Alberto stood on the runway for a moment, enjoying the evening's warmth. It was good to be back in Italy. Away from the terrible English weather, all those grey clouds and that constant rain.

As they walked around the plane to the cargo hatch they didn't speak to one another. They had already discussed what to do. There was no need for conversation or consultation.

Alberto reached up and turned the lever.

He swung open the big door and peered into the dark cargo hold. In the shadow, he could see the big wooden crate, just where they'd left it.

Chapter Sixteen

Tim heard a noise. A click and a thud. Someone was opening the door of the cargo hold.

He'd already tried to open it himself, but it was locked from the outside.

He pushed himself back against the wall. He felt very vulnerable. He didn't have a weapon. He was small and weak, and he couldn't possibly protect himself against big men with guns.

He'd just have to hope he was cleverer than them.

There was another clunk and the door swung open. The two men clambered into the cargo hold. Both had pistols tucked into their belts. But neither of them was carrying Grk. And neither of them noticed the boy pressed against the wall by the doorway.

Tim didn't move. He hardly even breathed. He stood in the shadows, watching the two men walk down the gangway to the big wooden crate. For a terrible moment he thought they might open it and look inside. Instead they picked it up, cursing at the weight, and lugged it down the gangway towards the open door.

Tim held his breath until they'd gone past.

Once the twins climbed out of the plane he stood inside the dingy cargo hold, watching the two men struggle across the runway with the heavy wooden crate. By their car they paused for a moment, catching their breath, then hauled the crate into the boot.

Tim smiled for a moment, imagining their expression when they opened the crate and found the bags of tea inside. Then his expression went back to being serious as he worried about what to do next. How was he going to find Grk?

He waited till the two men had driven away, then clambered down the ladder onto the asphalt and looked around, wondering where on earth he was. He was exposed here, but he felt safe for the moment. In the darkness, no one would be able to see him.

Because he'd been unconscious for the first part of the flight, Tim didn't even know how long he had been inside the aeroplane. They might have been flying for twenty minutes or ten hours. They could be in Edinburgh or Bristol or Paris or New York or Moscow, or just about anywhere else in the world.

He looked around for clues, but the airport didn't tell him anything. Several planes and helicopters were parked on the runway. He could see a few low-level buildings which were probably storage sheds and warehouses.

Up ahead, a crowd had gathered. Tim could see a line of police and several TV crews. People were cheering and clapping, waving flags and banners. A celebrity must have landed at the airfield. A singer or a film star.

Yes, there she was. Illuminated by the lights from the TV cameras. A slim, elegant woman. Holding a dog on a lead.

And not just any dog.

A dog called Grk.

She must have arrived on this plane. She'd been visiting London and now had come home. This crowd had come to greet her.

Who was she? And why had she stolen Grk?

She must be rich. She had a private jet to fly her around the world, plus a big black limousine and a couple of cars waiting for her on the asphalt when she arrived.

She must be famous, otherwise all these people wouldn't have gathered here to cheer and applaud her arrival.

And she must be important. Otherwise she wouldn't be protected from the public by a line of police.

If she was so rich, famous and important, why did she need to steal Grk? Why would she send two of her thugs to grab him from his real owners? Why couldn't she buy a dog of her own?

Whoever she was, and why ever she'd stolen Grk, she was now taking her time to talk to people in the crowd, shaking hands and kissing cheeks, greeting her beloved fans.

When she's finished, thought Tim, she'll get in that limo and drive to her home or her hotel.

And she'll take Grk with her.

He could see several police officers standing nearby, guarding the crowd. Couldn't he ask them to help him?

No. Of course not. They were looking after this woman, whoever she was. If he asked them for help, they'd probably arrest him.

He had a phone in his pocket, the phone that he'd been given by Tony. He could ring the British police. Or he could ring his mum and ask for her help.

Perhaps he should ring her anyway, just to tell her where he was. She'd probably be worrying about him.

He thought about Max and Natascha. He could imagine what they would be feeling. How much they would be panicking about Grk.

He had to get Grk back. He had to reunite Max and Natascha with their dog. He couldn't waste time asking anyone for help. He'd have to do it himself.

There was only one thing to do. Only one way to do it. He'd have to follow that woman's car.

But how?

He could see the driver standing by his door, smoking a cigarette and watching his boss, whoever she was.

Could he sneak past him and get into the car?

That wouldn't work. As soon as the woman came back to the car she'd notice him sitting in her seat.

How about opening the boot and hiding in there?

At least he'd be sure to go wherever she was going.

There were police standing nearby but none of them were looking this way. Even if they did they might not see him in the gloom.

Tim moved quickly across the asphalt.

To his relief, the driver didn't bother turning round to keep an eye on his car. But then, why would he? He wasn't expecting a small boy to sneak across the runway behind him, pop open the boot of the limousine, clamber inside and pull the lid shut after him.

Chapter Seventeen

Tim lay in the boot, waiting for the car to start. He hoped no one would come and put their luggage in here. If they did they'd see him immediately. He tried to imagine what he would do if the boot opened. Try and fight? Or just smile and pretend the whole thing was an embarrassing mistake?

Luckily the luggage must have been going in a different car, because he soon heard the sound of doors slamming, followed by the roar of the engine coughing into life.

As the limousine moved forward, the boot filled with acrid exhaust fumes. Tim couldn't help coughing. He put his hand over his mouth to stop himself making any more noise; he didn't want the passengers to hear him. He lay very still, breathing slowly, hoping enough oxygen would get in here among all the exhaust fumes.

He could hear a chorus of shouts and cheers, which gradually faded, and the whine of two sirens, one ahead and the other behind. A police escort, Tim decided, protecting the car's occupants. But from who? And why?

After what felt like fifteen or twenty minutes the car came to a stop and the engine was turned off.

He could hear voices and the slamming of doors. He listened for the sound of a small dog growling and snarling and trying to bite anyone within reach, but he couldn't hear Grk at all. Perhaps they've taped up his mouth, thought Tim. Or perhaps they've doped him.

The voices faded.

He listened to the silence for a minute or two, waiting till he was sure that everyone had gone, then shifted himself around and tried to get out of the car.

That was when he realised that he'd made a very stupid mistake.

Car boots aren't designed to be opened from the inside.

He wasted some time pushing the lid, and some more fiddling with the lock, searching for a catch, and yet more time trying to force up the lid, pushing it with his arms and legs, before accepting that he was stuck.

What could he do?

He could stay here, keeping quiet, waiting for them to come back. He'd have to hope that the limousine's owner, whoever she might be, was planning to drive away in the same car.

No, he didn't want to do that. Those two thugs would soon discover that he'd tricked them and escaped from the wooden crate. They'd come back and search for him. If they found him in here, he wouldn't have a chance of escaping again. And this time, they'd make no mistakes.

What else could he do?

He shouted.

No one answered.

He banged his fist on the side of the car.

No one came to help him.

He wondered where the car was parked. What if they were in the middle of the countryside? Or a basement garage? What if no one was anywhere near? What if he was trapped in here till the two thugs came back?

He tried again, banging his fists against the metal and shouting for help, yelling at the top of his voice. Even if the car was parked in a basement someone might be walking past to collect their own car. If they heard bangs and screams coming from a limousine, surely they'd come to investigate.

He heard a noise.

Someone was opening the boot.

No: someone was trying to open the boot. But they didn't have a key. He could hear voices. And footsteps. They were walking away. Leaving him here. He banged on the boot again, even harder this time, and yelled at the top of his voice. 'Help me! Please, help me! I'm stuck in here! Someone, please, come and help me!'

Suddenly the boot was opened. Bright light flooded in. Someone was shining a torch at him.

Tim sat up, shielding his eyes, and said, 'Can you turn that off?'

The torch beam shifted. He could see now.

Two men were staring down at him. They were wearing black caps and black uniforms with shiny silver buttons. Guards, he presumed.

Tim said, 'Where am I?'

The two men stared blankly at him.

Tim climbed out of the boot. He stretched his limbs and took a couple of deep breaths of the clean air, then smiled at the two men. 'Have you seen a lady with a dog?'

The guards just stared at him.

'I'm looking for a lady,' said Tim. 'With a dog. Have you seen her?'

The two men carried on staring at him.

'Oh, come on,' said Tim. 'You know what a dog is, don't you? *Woof, woof? Woof, woof?* Have you seen a woof-woof?' He growled and barked and showed his teeth just like a dog, which seemed to do the trick.

The two men giggled. One of them growled back at him, which wasn't very helpful. The other pointed at a nearby doorway and said something in a language that Tim couldn't understand.

'They went through there?' asked Tim.

The guards nodded.

'Great. Thanks for your help.'

Tim made for the door. But before he could get anywhere near it, the guards stopped him, each grabbing one of his arms.

'Let go,' said Tim, trying to pull himself free, but they were much stronger than him.

Holding him tightly, the guards called over one of their colleagues, a woman in a black suit.

'I can help you?' she asked in a strong foreign accent.

'You could ask these guys to let me go.'

The woman spoke to the men. They let him go.

'Thanks,' said Tim.

The woman said, 'Please, you will tell me, I can help you?'

'I want to go in there,' Tim told her, nodding at the door. 'But these guys won't let me.'

'It is not possible,' said the woman.

'Why not?' Tim asked.

'Because this is the door for the VIPs. You understand VIP?'

'You mean, very important people?'

'Yes, this is correct. Inside this door is only for the very important persons.'

'Who?' asked Tim.

'Excuse me?'

'Who is on the other side of that door?'

'I tell you already, sir. On the other side of the door is the very important persons.'

'But who are they?'

'This I cannot tell you.'

'Why not?'

'Because they are very important. Now, please, you will enjoy the TuttoFood. Have some cheese. Have some sausage. But you must not to be bothering the very important persons.'

Tim could see that there was no point arguing. He could also see that there was no point trying to push past the woman and the two guards. They could stop him easily. So he smiled and said, 'Thank you,' and acted like a boy who has made a mistake and is very sorry and will behave himself perfectly from now on, so you don't have to worry any more, OK?

Then he ran round the building, searching for another way to get inside.

Chapter Eighteen

Hanging over the doorway, there was a huge banner printed with a single word in big black letters:

TUTTOFOOD

Tim hardly even noticed the banner. He certainly didn't stop to read it or wonder what those nine letters might mean. He just ran through the doors and into the main lobby, which was packed with people. He looked around, wondering where to go next. How could he get to the VIP lounge?

Behind a long reception desk, six women in black suits were taking names and handing out tags and passes. At the next set of doors, guards in uniforms were checking tickets, making sure that no one came inside who hadn't paid and registered.

TuttoFood is the biggest and best exhibition of food anywhere in Italy. And, because Italians care more about their food than any other people from any other country, there isn't a bigger or better food exhibition anywhere on the planet. If you love food there is nowhere better than TuttoFood. The entire place is crammed with salamis, cheeses, pastas, puddings, breads, wine and all the other wonderful food and drink produced up and down the length of Italy. You can arrive thin and leave fat, having spent the whole day stuffing yourself.

But if you want to go inside you need a ticket.

And Tim didn't have one. Or any way of getting one.

When he tried to march through the gates, a uniformed guard stopped him and said something in a language that he couldn't understand.

'I don't know what you're saying,' said Tim. 'But can I get past, please? Some bad people have stolen my dog and I need to get him back.'

'Inglish?' said the guard.

'That's right. I'm English. And I've got to get my dog back.'

'Dogback? What is dogback?'

'I want to get my dog back.'

'No dogs,' said the guard. '*Non ammessi.*'

'No dogs?' repeated Tim.

'*Si.* No dogs.'

'Oh. I'm sorry. I didn't realise. Thanks for your help.' Tim smiled.

The guard smiled back.

Tim half-turned as if he was about to walk away. Then he darted forward and ran past the guard.

A quicker man might have stopped him. But this guard had already been sampling some of the delicious wares on offer at TuttoFood. Throughout the day, whenever he had a break from his duties, he had been tasting the pastries, salami, cheeses and wines available, and they had slowed down his usually speedy reflexes. He reached for Tim, but he wasn't quick enough. The boy slipped under his arms and ran through the lobby.

The guard looked around. Had anyone seen him? If they had, he would have run after the boy, shouting for help from his colleagues. But no one appeared to have noticed what had happened, and he really didn't feel like running. His stomach was much too full. Instead, he stayed at his post, smiling at the visitors and checking more tickets, waiting for his next break when he could try some more pasta. It was his supper time and he was getting hungry again. He'd smelt some fabulous lasagne on one of the stalls, and he could hardly wait to sample a spoonful or two, washed down with a glass of good red wine. A moment later he'd forgotten all about that annoying English boy and his dogback.

Chapter Nineteen

As soon as Tim entered TuttoFood he saw the woman who had stolen Grk. There was only one problem: about ten thousand people stood between her and him.

She was standing on a wooden stage. Grk was squatting at her feet. Two men were standing nearby. One of them was holding a large sausage. The other had a gold medal in one hand and a microphone in the other. He was talking to the crowd. Tim couldn't understand a word that he was saying, but everyone else obviously could, and they were loving it, cheering and applauding every few moments.

Who was he? What was he talking about? Why was the other man holding a sausage? And, most importantly, how were they connected to the woman who had stolen Grk?

Don't worry about all that now, Tim told himself. Just get closer to them and everything will make sense soon.

He hurried through TuttoFood, heading for the stage.

All around him chefs were serving a thousand different delicacies, putting them on plates to tempt anyone who happened to be walking past. There were tottering piles of salami and enormous hunks of crumbly cheese and warm beef stews and crispy chicken wings and thick bean soups and freshly fried fish and every imaginable variety of pasta. If you were at all hungry you would have been driven mad by all the fabulous foods on offer, and Tim was starving. He hadn't eaten since lunch, and that had been many hours ago. But he couldn't worry about that now. He could eat all he wanted later. First he had to get Grk back.

There was only one problem. Several thousand people stood between him and the stage, and none of them wanted to let him past. They were listening to the small man and they didn't want to give up their places. They weren't going to let a boy push past them. Especially a boy who couldn't even speak their language.

He said, 'Excuse me! Excuse me! Can I get past?'

But no one took any notice.

Wherever he went, whatever he did, however hard he pushed and shoved, he always found himself right where he'd started, standing at the back of the crowd, blocked behind a wall of bodies, unable to get any closer to the stage.

Up ahead the man with the sausage had left the stage. His place was taken by a woman with long strands of spaghetti dangling from both hands. The small man hung a gold medal around her neck and everyone applauded.

'*Ragazzo?*'

He heard a voice just behind him. It sounded like the voice of a girl, but he didn't know what she was saying, or even if she was talking to him, so he took no notice.

'*Ragazzo? Eh, ragazzo? Vuoi un po' di pizza?*'

Again Tim took no notice. He stood on tiptoes, trying to see over the top of the crowd, hoping for a sight of Grk.

Someone stepped in front of him.

It was a girl. She must have been about his age or perhaps a little older. She had brown eyes, black hair and a long, straight nose. She said, '*Ti piace la pizza?*'

'Excuse me,' replied Tim. 'You're blocking my view.'

He stepped aside, moving round the girl, peering through the scrum of bodies, looking for Grk.

'Where are you from?' asked the girl, speaking English with a strong accent.

Tim took no notice, but the girl didn't give up. She said, 'You are American?'

'No,' said Tim.

'So where are you from?'

'London.'

'Ah! *Inghilterra!* You are English?'

'Yes.' He didn't really mean to be rude but he didn't have time to talk to strange girls.

The girl was quiet for a moment. She didn't seem to understand that Tim didn't want to talk to her. Instead she said, 'You like pizza?'

Until now Tim had hardly even noticed that she was holding a slice of pizza in her right hand. He suddenly remembered that he hadn't eaten for a very long time. He nodded, unable to resist. 'Yes, I do like pizza.'

'You want?' She offered the pizza to him.

'Really? I can have it?'

'Go on, please. Is from the recipe of my family. This is the right word, *recipe*?'

'Yes,' said Tim.

'I hope you like.' The girl handed him the slice.

'Thank you.' He took a bite.

Over the years, Tim had eaten a lot of pizza.

Before Max and Natascha came to live with him, his mum and dad would always have a takeaway on Friday nights, and it would be often be a pizza from Mario's Special Deep-Pan Pizza Parlour, a takeaway not far from their home.

Until now Tim hadn't believed that pizza could get any better than the Four Seasons from Mario's.

He had been wrong. He suddenly knew that. Compared to this slice of pizza, the super-sized Four Seasons from Mario's Special Deep-Pan Pizza Parlour tasted no better than a rolled-up newspaper soaked in tomato juice. This pizza was almost unbelievably delicious. The base was crispy and crunchy. The white cheese oozed into his mouth, followed by tangy tomato and spicy salami. Oh, it was magnificent.

Tim ate the lot. He licked his lips and his fingers. Then he said, 'Thank you. That was delicious. That was amazing. That was the best pizza I've ever eaten, it really was. Your recipe is perfect.'

'You want one more?'

'Yes, please,' said Tim.

'*Bene*. You wait here.'

Just behind them there was a long wooden table, piled high with balls of mozzarella cheese, bowls of ripe tomatoes and plates of pizza decorated with different toppings. Tim now realised that the girl must have been working behind this stall; she'd noticed him when he stood in front of her and tried to push through the crowd.

He wondered why there weren't any adults on the stall. Why was she alone? Didn't she have any parents? Who made the pizzas? Did she? Alone? But all these questions fled from his mind when the girl darted back to the stall, grabbed another slice of pizza and offered it to him. 'Here you go,' she said. 'This is *carciofi*. You know *carciofi*?'

'Artichoke,' said Tim, looking at the pizza and spotting the slices of vegetable nestling among the pulpy tomato and melted mozzarella.

'Enjoy,' said the girl.

'I'm sure I will,' said Tim. He took a bite of the pizza. It was just as delicious as the last piece. He ate the lot and licked his lips. Then he turned to the girl and asked, 'Can you tell me something, please. What country is this?'

'What do you mean?' said the girl.

'I mean, where am I?'

'You mean, *here*? Where you are *here*?'

'Exactly.'

The girl looked at Tim as if he was completely mad. 'You want to sit down?'

'No, thanks. I feel fine. Please, just tell me where I am.'

'You are in Italy. You know Italy?'

'Sure.'

'This is Italy. Where do you think you are?'

'I really didn't know,' said Tim. 'But I suppose it makes sense. Pizza is from Italy, isn't it?'

'Of course,' said the girl. 'You like *il Duca*?'

'What?'

'I say, you like *il Duca*?'

'What's *il Duca*? A type of pizza?'

'No, not pizza. *Il Duca* is him.' The girl pointed through the crowd at the small man who was standing on the stage, presenting yet another gold medal, this time to a woman who was carrying a plump chicken under her arm. '*Il Duca*. In English, the duke. You like him?'

'No.'

'No? Then why you watch him?'

'He's called the duke?' asked Tim.

'*Si, si,* he is the Duke of Macaroni. He is a politic man, you understand?'

'A politician?'

'*Si, si,* a politician. He will be prime minister of our country, maybe.'

'And who's she?' asked Tim, pointing at the woman who had stolen Grk.

'This is his wife, *la Duchessa*. You understand?'

'The duchess?'

'Si, si. *La Duchessa*. And there is her dog. You see her dog? His name is Peppi.'

'That's not Peppi,' said Tim. 'That's Grk.'

'Grk? What you mean, Grk?'

Before Tim could answer, a wave of rapturous applause swept TuttoFood. The duke had given the final medal to the last of the prize-winners. Now he was waving to the crowd, and they were cheering back at him, showing their love, their adoration, their determination that he should be their next prime minister.

The cheers and applause continued for a few moments. Then the duke nodded to his wife. She walked off the stage, taking Grk, and the duke went after her. They were immediately surrounded by police and bodyguards, and ushered towards the nearest exit.

'I've got to go,' said Tim. 'Thanks again for the pizza. Bye.'

'Wait! I want to know—'

But Tim had already gone.

The girl stared after him. She picked up a slice of pizza, nibbled at the corner and wondered why such a nice-looking boy should be so interested in the Duke of Macaroni.

Chapter Twenty

Antonio and Alberto drove for about forty minutes along the motorway, leaving the airport and Rome far behind, then took a small road that snaked into the hills.

They had been this way before, several times, when they needed to dispose of things that should never be found. The road led through a village, past two farms and into a thick woodland which belonged to a friend of a friend of a friend of the Duke of Macaroni's. This friend of a friend of a friend knew that his woodland housed a few unpleasant secrets, but he didn't mind. He was always happy to help his friends. So he never came to his woodland, and he made sure that no one else did either. He built a big fence around the edge of the woods, and posted notices which said KEEP OUT and TRESPASSERS WILL BE PROSECUTED. Then he tried to forget that he had ever owned the woodland, and hoped no one would ever find whatever might be buried there.

Antonio and Alberto drove up a bumpy track that led through the middle of the woods and stopped in a clearing. They opened the doors of their car and stepped out. Around them, there was nothing to be seen except trees and nothing to be heard except birdsong.

Antonio said. 'You ready?'

'I'm ready,' replied his brother. 'How about you?'

'Of course I'm ready. Otherwise I wouldn't have asked if you were ready.'

'Then stop talking so much and let's do it.'

They walked to the back of the car.

Antonio unlocked it.

Alberto opened it.

They reached inside and wrapped their arms around the big wooden box, then hauled it out and placed it on the ground.

Antonio took a crowbar from the tool kit in the back of the car.

Alberto reached into the holster under his jacket and pulled out his gun. He hadn't fired a shot today, but that didn't matter. He checked it again. The magazine was full. He raised the gun, ready to fire, and nodded to his brother. 'Open it up.'

Antonio inserted the crowbar under the box's lid and pushed.

The lid flipped open.

Alberto sprang forward and, without taking the time to aim, fired six shots into the bottom of the box.

Bang! Bang! Bang! Bang! Bang! Bang!

A cloud of little black specks rose out of the crate and fluttered around Alberto's face.

He blinked, coughed, spluttered and waved away the tea leaves. Then he shone a torch into the bottom of the crate. When he saw what was there he holstered his gun, turned to his brother and said, 'We gotta problem.'

Chapter Twenty-One

The Duke and Duchess of Macaroni had a very busy schedule and they were running late. The duke had presented the prizes at TuttoFood, earning himself a few more votes for the elections. Now they had to get home to prepare for a much more important event, the speech that he would be giving tomorrow. They made their way through TuttoFood, shaking hands and kissing cheeks, eating little bites of cheese and pasta, taking tiny sips of coffee and wine, moving closer and closer towards the exit.

Their bodyguards went with them. So did the journalists who were taking photos for the following morning's newspapers, and the cameramen who were filming the scene for that evening's broadcasts, and the tourists who wanted to catch a glimpse of the next Prime Minister of Italy, and *il Duca*'s fans who wanted to catch a glimpse of their hero.

Grk went with them too.

Anywhere else, Grk would have been able to smell Tim, and would have gone straight to him. But here, in the middle of TuttoFood, Grk's nostrils were assaulted by scents from every side. His nose was bombarded by bubbling cauldrons of minestrone soup and heaving piles of mozzarella cheese and great plates of ravioli stuffed with spinach and about a billion other lovely smells, confusing him so much that he hardly knew where he was, and certainly couldn't distinguish one familiar scent among them all.

Even so, he could have tried to run away.

He could have sunk his teeth into the duchess's ankle and, when she screamed and threw up her hands in horror, darted into the crowd.

If that didn't work, he could even have bitten through his lead. His teeth were strong and sharp enough.

Instead he trotted calmly and quietly alongside the duchess, never making any kind of fuss.

Grk was a very loyal dog and he owed all his loyalty to three people who were not here. If they had been, he wouldn't have hesitated for a moment. If he had seen Tim, Natascha or Max all thoughts of doggy treats, however delicious, would have fled from his mind, and he would have sprinted towards them, desperate to escape from his captors and hurl himself into the arms of his beloved owners.

But Tim, Natascha or Max were nowhere to be seen.

And a woman kept offering him the most delicious snacks that he had ever tasted.

So he followed her obediently, hoping to be given one or two or maybe even three more of those yummy doggy treats.

Chapter Twenty-Two

Up ahead Tim could see the duke and duchess walking out of TuttoFood. The police and their bodyguards were holding back the crowds. A few more seconds and they would be gone for ever. If he was going to catch them, he had to do it now.

But he was stuck at the back of a heaving crowd, unable to get any closer. Bodies blocked his way. Hundreds of people were pushing forward. Everyone wanted to touch the duke. Everyone wanted to shake his hand. Everyone wanted to wish him luck in the elections. No one wanted to let a boy get past.

Tim couldn't see Grk, but he knew where he must be. Down on the ground. Out of sight. With a collar around his neck, and a lead attached to the collar, and the other end of the lead in that woman's hand.

Now the duke and duchess were saying their final goodbyes and walking out of TuttoFood, heading down the steps to their limousine. The crowd pushed after them, surging through the door, trying to get a final glimpse of their hero. Tim was taken with them. He couldn't go faster than the crowd. He couldn't go slower, either.

A long flight of stairs led down to the duke's big, black, bullet-proof limousine. A line of policemen stood between the crowd and the car, preventing anyone from getting too close.

One of their bodyguards opened the door.

For a moment Tim caught sight of a small white dog leaping up from the ground and into the back of the car.

He yelled at the top of his voice: 'GRK!'

Grk didn't hear him. Over the noise of the crowd he could hardly even hear himself.

Tim felt crazy with frustration. He was so close, but not close enough. He could see the duchess stepping into the car after Grk and settling herself on the back seat.

The duke paused to give a final wave, then clambered into the car after his wife. Once he was safely inside, their bodyguard shut the door.

The chauffeur started the engine and drove away.

Tim stood on the steps, squished in the middle of a large crowd, watching the limousine drive down the road.

He'd made a terrible mistake.

He should have stayed in that limo. He would have got a free trip to wherever they were going now.

He had no way to follow them. He couldn't push through the crowd. Even if he did the police would stop him. And even if he somehow managed to slip past them and run down the street he wouldn't be able to catch a car.

The limousine turned the corner. Its lights glimmered one last time. And then it was gone.

Tim felt desolate. He'd messed up. He'd made a terrible mistake. He'd been *this close* to getting Grk back again – and now Grk was out of reach.

He now knew who had dognapped Grk. The duchess. The wife of the Duke of Macaroni. It's a strange name, thought Tim. And then he thought, it's probably not so strange if you're Italian. It probably sounds entirely normal.

But why would a duchess want to kidnap Grk?

He'd like to ask her exactly that.

But he'd have to find to her first.

He didn't know why she and her husband had taken Grk, or where they had gone, or how to find them again. He couldn't imagine that anyone would help him, either. If he went to the police they'd just laugh at him. He was a boy, and a foreigner, and he couldn't speak their language. Why would they help him track down a powerful politician?

So what could he do? He wanted to track down Grk, but he didn't even know where to start looking. He had no money. And he had no idea where the duke and duchess might have gone. What could he do? How could he find them?

Suddenly he had an idea. He thought of someone who might be able to help him.

He turned round and hurried back inside.

Chapter Twenty-Three

To his relief the girl was still there, standing behind her stall, offering pieces of pizza to passers-by. When she saw Tim, she smiled and said, '*Ciao. Come stai?*'

'I don't know what that means,' said Tim.

'It means, "How are you?".'

'Oh. I'm fine, thanks.'

'*Bene*. That means "good". *Come si dice?*'

'What does that mean?'

'It means, "what is your name?".'

'Tim.'

'Hello, Tim. I am Alessandra.'

'Pleased to meet you, Alessandra.'

'I am pleased to meet you too, Tim. You want one more pizza?'

'I'd love one,' said Tim. 'Thanks.'

Alessandra selected a large slice and handed it to him.

He took a big bite, chewed and swallowed. 'Delicious,' he said. 'Did you make it?'

'*Il mio papà*, my father, he makes the mozzarella. *Il fornaio del nostro villaggio*, the baker in our village, we deliver to him the mozzarella and he is making the pizza for us. You know mozzarella?'

'The cheese?' said Tim.

'*Si,* the cheese. We have a farm. We have many of the *bufala*. Excuse me, but what is the *bufala* in English?'

'Buffalo, I guess.'

'Ah, yes, buffalo. My family, we have a farm. My father, he is the farmer. We have many of the buffalo. From their milk, we are making mozzarella. We have come here to TuttoFood for my father to be meeting the restaurants. He is there now.' Alessandra waved her hand vaguely, suggesting that her father was somewhere out there, carrying samples of his cheese. 'And you? Why are you here in TuttoFood? You are a lover of the food?'

'I told you already,' said Tim. 'I've come to find my dog.'

'Ah, yes. Your dog. The one who is not Peppi, yes? Gruk? That is his name, yes?'

'His name is Grk,' said Tim.

'Grk,' repeated the girl, echoing his pronunciation. 'So, why did *il Duca* want to take your Grk?'

'I don't know. That's what I'm here to find out. For some reason, his wife has stolen him.'

'*Il Duca* stole your dog?'

'Yes?'

'How? When? Why?'

'If you really want to know, I'll tell you,' said Tim. 'But I have to warn you, it's a long story.'

'*Bene,*' said the girl. 'I like stories very much. Please, come here, sit. You can tell me all.'

Tim sat beside her on the wooden bench behind the stall and told her about going to the museum that afternoon with his mum, Max and Natascha, then seeing two men looking through the car window at Grk.

The girl interrupted him. She wanted to know who Max and Natascha were.

'They're Grk's owners,' said Tim.

'The dog, he is belonging to them?'

'Yes.'

'Not to you?'

'No.'

'Then why are you here in Roma? Why are you chasing a dog who is not yours?'

To explain that, Tim had to explain everything. He told her about the day that he had been walking home from school, dreaming about his computer, and had tripped over a dog in the street. He explained how he had run away from home and flown to Stanislavia and rescued the Raffifis from prison and brought them and Grk back to London. (If you don't already know the full details of this story, you should read *A Dog Called Grk.*)

He also told her about his and Grk's adventures around the world. He described how they had tracked down the Pelotti Brothers in Brazil, rescued the Golden Dachshund in New York, outwitted Edward Goliath in the Seychelles, smashed the Blue Rat Gang in Delhi, defeated the Red Jelly Gang in Sydney, and taken revenge on Colonel Zinfandel in Paris.

Finally he described how those two identical men had grabbed Grk, and how he had followed them and been bashed over the head, and now come here.

He was worried that Alessandra might not believe him. If someone had told him the same story, he probably wouldn't have believed it himself. But to his surprise, although she asked a few questions, she obviously believed every word that he said.

When he had finished explaining how he came to be here Alessandra said: 'Why do they steal your dog Grk? Why do they want to take him from you?'

Tim shrugged his shoulders. 'I suppose it must be something to do with him looking like Peppi, but I don't know. To be honest, I don't really care. I just want to get him back again. But I've got a problem. The duke, *il Duca*, has taken him away, but I don't know where they've gone. Can you help me find him?'

'You must come talk to my papa,' said Alessandra. 'He will help you. My papa, he hates *il Duca*. He says he is the worst thing that will happen to Italy. He says the duke is a bad man. He says if the duke is prime minister it will be all big problems for Italy. If you have problem with *il Duca*, you must talk to *il mio papà*, he will help you. Come, we can find him and tell him everything, and he will help you.'

Tim shook his head. 'I don't think it's a good idea.'

'Why not?'

'I've never met your father, but I bet I know just what he'll say. He'll tell us that we're being silly. He'll say we should leave it to the police. And, worst of all, he'll want to call my mum and dad, and tell them where I am.'

'They don't know?'

'No,' said Tim. 'And I don't want them to know. If they find out I'm here, they'll call the police, or the British embassy, and get someone to stop me doing anything. Then I'll never find Grk. Once I've got him back I'll tell them where I am.'

The girl nodded. 'You're right,' she said. 'My father, he is the same. He will say you are too young. He will say you are only a boy. He will say you cannot do nothing yourself. All the time he is saying these things to me.'

'That's why I need *your* help,' said Tim. 'Not your father's.'

'No problem,' smiled Alessandra. 'What do you want me to do?'

Chapter Twenty-Four

A tall, bearded man came through the crowds of Tutto-
Food, carrying a large bag of cheese. He was looking
tired and depressed. Hardly glancing at Alessandra, and
not even noticing Tim, he dumped his bag on the table,
slumped into a chair and sighed.

'*Ciao, Papà,*' said Alessandra brightly.

'*Ciao,*' replied her father with another sigh. He was in
a bad mood. His day had not been successful. He had
been walking around TuttoFood from early that morning
until now, late evening, carrying a tray of the soft, fresh,
delicious mozzarella, made from the milk of his own
buffalos. He had been offering samples to chefs and
restauranteurs, but very few of them were interested.
They might have come all the way to TuttoFood because
they adored food, but today they didn't want to talk
about cheese. They just wanted to talk about the Duke of
Macaroni and his ridiculous plans for Italy.

'*Papà?*' said Alessandra.

'*Si?*'

'This is my friend Tim,' she told her father. 'He is
coming from London.'

Salvatore Pecorino looked up. For the first time he
noticed the boy sitting beside his daughter. He smiled.
'*Ciao, Tim. Come stai?*'

'I'm fine, thanks,' said Tim. 'But I don't speak Italian.'

'*Scusi*, I don't speak no good English,' said Alessandra's father. 'But my daughter, she is good English, yes?'

'Very good,' said Tim.

Alessandra said, 'Papa, he needs our help.'

'Help? What help?'

'He needs our help to find his parents.'

'*In Italiano, per favore*,' instructed her father.

Just as he had asked, Alessandra talked to him in Italian. She explained that Tim was staying in Rome with his mother and father. The three of them had been visiting TuttoFood together that evening. They had gone back to their hotel in different taxis and each of them must have thought Tim was with the other. If Tim could get there before them the family would be reunited without any tears, but one thing stood in his way. He had no money. Could they lend him enough to pay for the taxi?

None of this was true, of course, and Alessandra didn't like saying it to her father. She hated lying to him. But she knew that Tim was right: if she had admitted the truth her father would have insisted on phoning Tim's parents in London, telling them everything and keeping their son safe until they could come and collect him.

Luckily Alessandra's father didn't ask any awkward questions. He simply pulled out his wallet and handed over fifty euros. He'd never met Tim before, and didn't know anything about him, but that wasn't important. If his daughter trusted Tim and wanted to help him, then Salvatore Pecorino wanted to help him too.

'Thank you very much,' said Tim. He turned to Alessandra. 'How do you say that in Italian?'

'*Grazie* means thank you,' said Alessandra. 'For to say thank you many times, you can say *grazie mille.*'

'*Grazie mille,*' said Tim, trying to echo his new friend's pronunciation.

'*Prego,*' said Salvatore Pecorino. Which means more or less the same as 'it's my pleasure' in English. Then he sprang to his feet and smiled at two women who had stopped beside the stall, wanting to inspect the mozzarella on display and taste a piece of pizza.

While her father was talking to the women, telling them about his herd of buffalo, Alessandra borrowed his phone. She quickly connected to the internet and looked up the Duke of Macaroni's schedule, trying to find out where he would be staying that night.

She discovered the information very quickly. It was no secret. In 1834 the first Duke of Macaroni bought a plot of land in Rome and built himself a large, elegant and very expensive mansion. The Macaronis had lived there ever since. When the duke was in Rome, he would stay nowhere else.

Once Alessandra had learned what she needed to know she tugged her father's arm and told him that she was going to take Tim to the taxi rank at the front of TuttoFood. He couldn't speak any Italian, she said, so she needed to put him in a taxi and tell the driver where to go.

'*Arrivederci,*' said Salvatore Pecorino. '*Buona fortuna.*'

'That means goodbye,' explained Alessandra. 'And good luck.'

'*Grazie mille,*' called Tim.

Chapter Twenty-Five

Tim and Alessandra pushed their way through the crowds of TuttoFood and emerged through the main exit.

A line of taxis was waiting at the bottom of the stairs. There wasn't a queue. People simply pushed forward and thrust themselves into the nearest taxi.

Alessandra might have been small and skinny, but she was as good at queue-jumping as anyone else, and she soon managed to nab a taxi for Tim. Without her he would have stood at the back of the crowd for hours and never got a taxi. She opened the door, poked her head inside and talked to the driver, telling him where to go.

Tim sat on the back seat. He waved to Alessandra. 'Thank you,' he said. 'Thank you for everything.'

He was expecting her to say goodbye and slam the door. Instead, to his surprise, she got in after him and then slammed the door. The driver started the engine. A moment later they were driving away from TuttoFood and heading across the city.

'What are you doing?'

'I come too,' Alessandra answered.

'Where?'

'For to find Grk.'

'Why?'

'You don't speak no Italian. You don't know nothing about Roma. How are you going to find Grk without me?'

'I thought you told your father you were just going to show me to the taxi rank and put me in a taxi?'

'This is exactly what I tell him,' said Alessandra with a broad smile.

'What's he going to think when you don't come back? Won't he be worried?'

'It is no problem.'

'Of course it is!'

'Why so?'

'Because he'll be worried about you. He won't know where you are. You have to go back.'

'You tell me, you do it, just the same. When you go to Stanislavia with Grk and find Max and Natascha.'

'That's different,' Tim insisted.

'Why is it so different?'

'Because . . . Because . . . Because it is.'

'I don't think so,' said Alessandra. 'I think it is the same.'

Tim wanted to argue with her, but he couldn't. She was right. Just like her, he had run away from his parents to rescue Grk, leaving a note to tell them where he was going. In fact, he'd done more or less the same thing again today. Why should Alessandra behave any differently?

'Fine,' he said. 'You can come with me if you want to. But don't blame me if it's dangerous.'

'I don't blame you for nothing.' Alessandra smiled as if nothing could possibly make her happier than a bit of danger to spice up an otherwise ordinary evening.

Chapter Twenty-Six

The Palazzo Macaroni was surrounded by high walls topped with coils of barbed wire and security cameras. A huge steel gate guarded the entrance. Four armed men stood beside the gate, checking the identities of anyone who wanted to come inside.

When a couple of kids wandered past, the guards hardly even glanced at them. Why should they? They had been hired to protect the duke and duchess from terrorists and journalists, not children.

Not wanting to arouse any suspicion, Alessandra had asked the taxi to drop them in the next street rather than right outside the palazzo's main entrance. Now, she and Tim walked slowly past, glancing at the gate and the guards, before following the line of the walls.

They walked all the way around the Palazzo Macaroni, searching for another way in, and soon found themselves back where they had started, at the big steel gate.

This was the only entrance. There was no other way to get into the Palazzo Macaroni. If they were going to get in there and rescue Grk, they would have to outwit the armed men and sneak through a gate four times as tall as themselves.

Tim heard the growl of an engine. He turned round and saw a big black car driving down the street. In the light cast by the street lamps, Tim recognised the two men in the front seats. In a moment they would recognise him too. Turning away so they could only see the back of his head, he hissed to Alessandra, 'That's them!'

'That's who?'

'The dognappers. In that car. They mustn't see me.'

'Pretend you are talking to me,' said Alessandra.

They stood, pretending to have a conversation, while Tim faced away from the car and Alessandra told him what it was doing.

She described how the car stopped by the main gate, and the driver wound down his window and chatted to the guards, laughing and talking as if they were old friends.

If the dognappers had been looking out for Tim they might have recognised his clothes, even if they couldn't see his face, but they ignored him.

One of the guards lifted a walkie-talkie to his mouth and gave some instructions. A moment later the heavy steel gate slid open and the car drove inside, taking the dognappers into the Palazzo Macaroni.

'They've gone,' said Alessandra.

Tim turned just in time to see the gate sliding shut, blocking the entrance. The car had vanished. So had the dognappers.

He stared at the guards, the gate and the high walls, wondering what to do. He felt intensely frustrated. If he could only think of some way to get inside the Palazzo Macaroni. But how?

He went through the possibilities in his mind and dismissed each of them.

He couldn't disguise himself; the guards would never be fooled by him.

He couldn't smash down the walls or the gate; he didn't have a bulldozer or a tank.

He couldn't climb over the walls; he didn't have a ladder – and even if he found one, he would immediately be spotted on the CCTV cameras. The darkness wouldn't help him; there would be searchlights everywhere, guarding the palazzo from thieves and terrorists.

He couldn't fly over them, either; he didn't have a helicopter or any way of getting one.

So what could he do? How could he rescue Grk?

Chapter Twenty-Seven

Inside the Palazzo Macaroni the Duke of Macaroni was talking to six of his closest and most trusted advisers, planning his speech for the following day. He had practised it again and again, making sure that every word was perfect, but he still wasn't satisfied. He knew that this was the most important speech of his life. One mistake might be enough to ruin his political career. He turned from one adviser to the next, asking for their suggestions. They had written the speech for him. Now he wanted them to make it even better.

No one noticed the door opening. No one saw Alberto and Antonio slipping through the doorway and standing at the edge of the room, waiting to be noticed. They probably would have stood there all night if Alberto hadn't coughed twice, loudly, drawing attention to himself.

The duke glanced at his bodyguards, then muttered to his advisers, excusing himself for a moment and ordering them to continue working on his speech. He hurried down the long room to Antonio and Alberto. When he reached them he said, 'I'm rather busy, boys. Is it important?'

'Yes, boss,' said Antonio.

'We done what you wanted, boss,' explained Alberto.

Before replying, the duke glanced down the room to check that no one would be able to hear what he was saying. 'He's gone?'

'He's gone,' confirmed Antonio.

'No one will ever find him?'

'Never,' said Alberto.

'Thank you, my friends. You have proved yourselves yet again. When I win the elections you will have your just reward. I'm planning to give you both good posts in the government. You will be my Minister for Security, Alberto. And you, Antonio, you will be Minister for Police.'

'Thanks, boss,' said Antonio.

'Yeah, thanks, boss,' said Alberto.

Neither of them particularly wanted to be ministers, but they were looking forward to all the perks that went with the job: the big cars, the big houses, the big salaries and the long lunches. After years of doing dirty work for their boss, they would finally be able to relax and enjoy themselves.

The duke was just about to go back to his advisers when Antonio said, 'Er, boss?'

'Yes?'

'What about Peppi?'

'What about him?'

'You wanna we deal with him too?'

'No, no. Peppi's fine. He's with my wife. They're upstairs, eating chocolates and reading magazines together.'

'But, boss...' said Alberto.

'Yes?'

'That's not Peppi. That's some other dog.'

The duke smiled. 'This morning that dog might have been some other dog. Now it's Peppi. And it will remain Peppi for the rest of its life. Do you understand?'

'Sure, boss,' said Antonio.

'No problem, boss,' said Alberto.

'I want you both to forget about the other dog,' the duke ordered. 'I'll forget about him too. Pretty soon, even that dumb dog will forget he's ever been anything except Peppi.'

Chapter Twenty-Eight

Dottore Marcello Ricotta was the best vet in Rome. He was forty-seven years old, a tall man with short grey hair and a distinguished face, and he had devoted his entire life to animals. Every day his surgery was packed with nervous owners wanting to know what was wrong with their cats, dogs, hamsters, lizards, toads or turtles.

Year by year Dottore Ricotta's reputation spread, until even the city's richest residents wanted his services. They would summon him to their houses, where he would peer down the throats of their beloved pets and try to answer their desperate questions. Did their pot-bellied pig have a tummy ache? Why was their newt not his usual self? Should their anaconda be taking more exercise?

Now Dottore Ricotta was cruising through the streets of Rome in his silver Mercedes, driving towards the home of his richest and most famous patient, a small black and white dog named Peppi.

An hour ago he had been relaxing after dinner, settling down to read the latest edition of his favourite magazine, *Vets in Action*. But when the duchess had rung and asked him to come to the Palazzo Macaroni he didn't even hesitate. He'd grabbed his bag and hurried to his car.

Dottore Ricotta had never actually visited Peppi before. The little dog was remarkably healthy and never needed the attention of a vet. But he knew all about him.

Every Roman did. Most Italians did too. Peppi was the most famous dog in the country. He belonged to the wife of the man who would soon be their prime minister.

When Dottore Ricotta arrived at the big steel gates outside the Palazzo Macaroni he wound down his window and gave his identity card to the guards. He had been summoned by the duchess, he explained, who wanted him to look at her dog.

The guards checked his face against his photograph and his name against a list of expected visitors, then one of them spoke into a walkie-talkie.

The big steel gate slid open.

Just as Dottore Ricotta was about to drive forward, there was a heart-rending scream. Startled, he looked around, wondering what had happened.

Not far away a young girl had fallen to the floor.

She was clutching her chest and crying for help.

Dottore Ricotta sprang out of his car and ran up the road to check if she was hurt.

The guards went with him.

If the Duke of Macaroni had seen them deserting their post he would have been furious, but they didn't worry about that. They might have been guards, but they were men too. They had families of their own, wives and daughters. If a girl fell to the ground, screaming for help, they couldn't just stand there and watch.

The guards crowded round the girl. Dottore Ricotta knelt on the pavement and talked to her in a calm, reassurring voice. 'Can you hear me?' he asked. 'Can you tell me where it hurts?'

None of them looked back at Dottore Ricotta's Mercedes.

None of them saw a boy opening one of the rear doors, clambering onto the back seat and slowly, quietly, closing the door after him.

After a few seconds the girl opened her eyes.

She blinked, looked around and asked what had happened.

'You fell down,' Dottore Ricotta told her. 'Don't you remember?'

The girl smiled and shook her head. She couldn't remember anything, she said.

Dottore Ricotta and the guards helped the girl to her feet. Miraculously, she didn't appear to be hurt. She brushed down her dress and thanked them for her help. She couldn't understand what had just happened, she said, but she felt perfectly fine now, and definitely didn't need to go to hospital. Thanking them again, she walked away.

When the girl had gone Dottore Ricotta and the guards looked at one another and shrugged their shoulders.

The guards returned to their posts. Dottore Ricotta returned to his car and drove into the Palazzo Macaroni. The big steel gates swung shut behind him.

Tim lay down in the back of the big silver car, hidden under a blanket, and tried not to make any noise. Luckily the drive was short. They went through the gates and along a road. Tim could hear the wheels scrunching on gravel. Then they turned a corner and came to a stop.

Tim heard the driver climbing out of the car and slamming his door. There was a loud *clickety-clunk* as the doors were locked from the outside. Footsteps walked away from the car.

Tim waited till he couldn't hear them any more then tugged the edge of the blanket away from his face.

All he could see was the back of the seat.

Slowly, cautiously, he sat up.

And raised his head.

And looked out of the window.

The car was parked between two other cars. In the gloom, he could barely make out the back of a man who was walking away from him.

He could have stayed where he was, waiting till the coast was clear, but Tim preferred the idea of following that man inside, using him to gain access to the palazzo.

The car's doors were locked, but that didn't stop them opening from the inside. Tim slid out and quietly closed the door, then darted through the lines of parked cars.

He followed his driver through a white door and up some stairs. He could see him just up ahead, talking to a man in a dark suit.

Tim didn't know which way to go. Should he hide? Or hurry through the house, searching for Grk?

Suddenly he heard a noise.

The sound of a dog yapping.

He recognised those yaps.

They were coming from upstairs.

The two men started climbing a wide stone staircase.

Tim went after them.

His footsteps resounded on the marble.

He stopped and slipped off his shoes. His socks wouldn't make any noise.

He hurried up one flight of stairs.

Then another.

Always keeping the men in sight.

They stopped at a door and knocked twice. A voice came from inside. The men opened the door and went into the room, leaving the door ajar.

Tim paused outside.

He could hear voices coming from inside the room. A woman was talking to two men.

Along with the voices, Tim could hear something else too. Something more familiar. Something that he hadn't heard all day.

Tim knew Grk's sounds very well. His barks, his growls, his squeals, his whines, his snuffles and his snores – Tim knew them all, and he knew what each of them meant. They were Grk's language, the way that he communicated with the world and the people around him.

Tim knew what Grk was saying now. He was whining and growling in a way which meant he wasn't happy at all. In a moment he'd probably lash out and bite the nearest ankle, whoever it belonged to.

If he could hear Grk, thought Tim, Grk would be able to hear him.

Tim whispered: 'Grk.'

Nothing happened. No one answered. But that wasn't surprising. He'd been speaking so quietly that he couldn't even hear himself.

He tried again, speaking a little louder. 'Grk.'

Through the open doorway he could still hear the sound of voices, and Grk's growls, which were getting a little louder.

He spoke once more, louder still: 'Grk.'

The voices carried on talking, but the growls stopped. Grk must have heard him.

Like all dogs, Grk had remarkably sensitive hearing.

'Grk,' whispered Tim once more. 'Come here, boy.'

Chapter Twenty-Nine

Dottore Marcello Ricotta knelt on the floor and stroked Peppi's ears. 'Hello, old chap,' he said. 'I hear you're not feeling well.'

Grk wagged his tail. He didn't know what this man might be talking about, but he liked him. And trusted him too. With any luck this man would be able to get him back to Tim, Natascha and Max.

Dottore Ricotta ran his hands along Grk's back, then lifted the dog's lips and peered at his teeth and tongue.

Carla, the Duchess of Macaroni, nervously watched what the vet was doing.

She had spent a very strange evening with her beloved Peppi.

She had always thought that there was no creature on the planet whom she knew better than her own dog. Not even herself.

But today he hadn't been himself.

He'd been restless. Impatient. Unhappy. Uncomfortable. And odd.

She couldn't understand what was wrong.

He usually spent hours on her lap or sitting beside her, happy to be near his mistress while she talked on the phone and discussed vital matters with her hairdresser, her manicurist, her gardeners or her interior designers. Today he only settled down when she offered him another of those treats. Unfortunately she'd run out of them earlier in the day. She sent an urgent message to the chef, ordering him to cook some more. The chef started work immediately, but the treats wouldn't be ready till the morning.

Without any treats to distract him, Peppi grew more and more uncomfortable. He whined, yapped and snarled. Carla began to worry that he might even bite her again.

Eventually she decided that he must be ill. She sent for the finest vet in Rome. According to one of her friends he was a magician with animals and could cure any kind of problem.

Peppi seemed to like him.

He allowed the vet to stroke him.

He didn't even mind when the vet looked inside his ears and mouth.

And then suddenly, for no apparent reason, Peppi jumped up and started barking.

He sprinted towards the door, his claws skittering on the polished marble floor.

'Peppi!' shouted the duchess. 'Peppi! Where are you going, Peppi?'

Peppi didn't stop. He didn't even pause. He just ran out of the room.

Tim heard the sound of four small paws pitter-pattering across cold white marble.

Then he heard a voice.

A woman's voice.

121

Shouting in Italian.

'*Peppi! Peppi! Dove vai, Peppi?*'

A small black and white shape streaked through the doorway, his ears upright on the top of his head, his tail wagging madly from side to side, and hurled himself into Tim's arms, almost knocking him off his feet.

'Urgh!' said Tim.

There isn't much else you can say when a small dog is licking your face.

He would have like to say a lot more. Even better, he would have liked to get down on the ground and tickle Grk's tummy. But he knew they didn't have time for conversation or tummy-tickling. They had to get out of there.

He put Grk on the floor and said, 'This way.'

Grk looked around, wagging his tail and barking happily.

Tim knew what he was saying. *Where's Max? Where's Natascha? When can I jump into their arms too?*

'Soon. Come on, this way.'

He ran towards the stairs, carrying his shoes. Grk galloped joyfully alongside him.

They were making lots of noise, their feet and paws smacking against the marble floors, but Tim didn't care about that now. There was no need to hide any more. They just had to get out of the Palazzo Macaroni as fast as possible.

Together, the boy and the dog sprinted down the wide marble staircase.

The duchess turned to the vet. 'What have you done to my dog?'

'I didn't, erm, I didn't do anything,' stammered Dottore Ricotta.

'You must have done something,' the duchess snapped. 'Because you scared him.'

'Perhaps he wasn't scared of me. Perhaps he's been scared by something else. Can you describe his symptoms? How has he been behaving today?'

Ignoring all these idiotic questions, the duchess turned on her heel and swept towards the door. 'I'll deal with you later,' she called over her shoulder to the vet. 'For now I've got to find Peppi.'

Tim and Grk ran down two flights of stairs and then stopped. Their way was blocked. At the bottom of the staircase three men were standing in the hallway, chatting and laughing. They hadn't seen him yet, but they would as soon as they turned their heads.

A shout came from higher in the house. 'Peppi! Peppi!'

The three men looked up.

Just in time Tim ducked back and pressed himself against the wall.

'Grk!' he hissed. 'Grk, come here.'

Grk wagged his tail and yapped.

Whoah! Whoah! Whoah whoah whoah!

For the first time all day Grk was having fun.

If Tim wanted to play a game, he'd be happy to play

too. He didn't understand the rules but that didn't matter. He never really understood the rules. He just ran around and barked a lot. So that was what he did now.

'*Shh!*' hissed Tim.

Grk barked even louder.

Tim looked around. He could hear shouting from upstairs and downstairs. The duchess was on her way. So were those three men. In a moment they'd meet in the middle, trapping him here.

He noticed an open door.

'This way,' he whispered and dodged through the doorway.

Grk wagged his tail even more enthusiastically and ran after him.

On the other side of the door they found themselves in a large white room. Big paintings hung on the walls. There was an enormous gold chandelier hanging from the middle of the ceiling. Three huge sofas surrounded a vast fireplace.

Tim looked about, wondering what to do now. There was another door leading out of the room on the other side. Should he run through there? Or hide in here? Could he snuggle under a sofa? Or clamber up the fireplace? Could he and Grk conceal themselves in the chimney? That might be the perfect place to wait for an hour or two. But if they hid in a chimney, they'd be trapping themselves. Would that be a terrible mistake?

Then he remembered his shoes.

He was still carrying one in each hand. He slipped them on his feet. That was better. Now he could run properly.

He looked at Grk and said, 'What's that around your neck?'

Grk wagged his tail.

Tim knelt on the floor and unclasped the collar that had been strapped around Grk's neck. It was covered with small sparkling jewels. They looked like diamonds. They might have been worth millions, but Tim didn't care. He didn't want to steal someone else's diamonds. He just want to find Grk's collar again and strap it back on.

He stood up. 'Right, Grk. Which way shall we go?'

At that moment the far door opened and two men stepped into the room.

They stared at Tim for a moment. Then both of them reached into their holsters and pulled out their guns.

Chapter Thirty

Down in the kitchen Antonio and Alberto had been eating fried chicken, ripping the bird from its bones with their bare hands, and licking their fingers after every bite. It was delicious. After several days of dreary English food, nothing tasted better than some real Italian meat.

But when they heard the shouts coming from upstairs, they didn't hesitate. They pushed their plates away and sprang to their feet.

The Gorgonzola twins were the duke's bodyguards. They did all kinds of other jobs for him too, but above all they were paid to protect him. What were those shouts? Was someone attacking their boss? Had terrorists or assassins broken into the palazzo? There was only one way to find out. They wiped their hands on their shirts, drew their weapons and ran up the back stairs.

When they went into the main drawing room, the first thing they saw was a dog.

Not just any dog – that ungrateful mutt who had been causing them so much trouble all day.

Then they saw the boy.

The boy who should have been buried in a shallow grave in a forest where he would never be found.

But here he was. Not buried. Not even dead. Running around the Palazzo Macaroni as if he owned the place, his dog with him.

Antonio and Alberto knew what would happen if the duke saw the boy. He would kill them. There was only one way to stop him. They'd have to kill the boy first and put him where he belonged. In a hole in the ground in the forest, buried where no one would find him.

Alberto and Antonio lifted their arms and pointed their guns at the boy.

Grk's ears shot into the air and stood upright on the top of his head.

He opened his mouth, showing his short, sharp teeth.

And he growled.

All day these two men had been bullying him. They'd grabbed him, stuffed him in a bag, beaten him, shouted at him and taken him from the people that he loved most in the world.

Now he wanted revenge.

He darted forward, skidded round the side of the nearest sofa and hurled himself at the first leg that he saw.

Tim slowly lifted his hands in the air.

'Don't shoot,' he said. 'I surrender.'

What else could he do? He wasn't armed. He didn't know karate or judo. He couldn't possibly fight two men who had guns.

He was sure they couldn't shoot him here. They wouldn't want to get blood on the carpet. They'd have to take him away. Tim just had to hope that while they were doing it he'd be able to find some cunning way to wriggle out of their grasp and run off.

One of the men stepped forward, keeping his pistol aimed at Tim's head, and said something in Italian.

At exactly the same moment the other man screamed and jumped in the air, clutching his ankle.

Grk had just bitten him.

Now Grk whirled round and bit the first man too.

Both of them were hopping around the room, waving their arms and shouting.

Grk darted after them, trying to get his jaws buried in another of their ankles.

Both men were armed and could have shot him, but they didn't dare shoot the duchess's dog. They knew how she would react if she came into the room and saw Peppi on the floor, blood oozing from a deadly wound. He wasn't really Peppi, of course, but she wouldn't know that. So they danced about, waving their useless guns in the air, and Grk lunged after them, trying to get his jaws on their ankles.

While the men were dancing and Grk was lunging Tim took his chance and sprang at the door.

The two men whirled round and aimed their guns at him.

Then one of them yelped.

And the other yelled.

As Grk nipped their ankles once more.

Tim darted through the door. On the other side he shouted: 'GRK! COME HERE, GRK!'

He only had to wait for a moment then Grk streaked through the door, his eyes bright, his tail wagging, his teeth trailing scraps of cotton torn from the brothers' trousers.

Together, Tim and Grk ran down the narrow flight of stairs.

Behind him Tim could hear the two men shouting and cursing. Then he heard their footsteps thumping down the staircase, coming after him. He wanted to look round, but he knew he didn't have any time to waste.

At the bottom of the stairs he could see three doors.

He opened the nearest. It was a cupboard. The shelves were stacked with crockery and glasses.

He opened the next one. It led into a kitchen. A chef in a white apron was sprinkling herbs into a big pot.

Grk took a few deep sniffs. He would have been happy to go and investigate the smells but to his disappointment Tim shut the door and reached for the next one, the last one – the only remaining option.

Behind it, another flight of stairs led down into a basement or a cellar.

Tim could hear heavy footsteps. The two men were just behind him. They'd be here in a moment.

He ran down the stairs. Grk galloped alongside him.

At the bottom of the stairs they found a dusty wooden door, secured with three heavy bolts. Tim pulled them back and opened the door. The air was stale and musty. He could see the shadowy shapes of bottles stacked along the walls. This must be the wine cellar. Could he and Grk hide among them? Only if they found a cupboard or a cave. Only if they got there before the two men saw where they were going. Only if—

He heard a bang. A bullet pinged across the room, smashing through several bottles. Glass rained down on the floor, followed by gushing wine. A heady stench filled the air.

Tim ducked and ran.

Grk sprinted alongside him.

They went down one corridor, then another. A swinging bulb cast wild shadows. Up ahead, Tim could see a wooden door. He wondered what lay on the other side. The walls were rougher here, and there were no more bottles. This part of the cellar obviously wasn't used. The air smelt of dust and neglect.

He tried the door. It was locked.

He heard footsteps again. He couldn't tell where they were coming from. He didn't know whether to keep going or turn round.

Down at his feet Grk growled, but even he didn't seem to know what he was growling at.

Not wanting to wait for them to come and get him, Tim started running. Grk ran alongside him.

They turned a corner and jogged down another long corridor. A few bricks had fallen from the roof and lay on the floor where they had dropped.

Then they came to a hole in the floor.

Tim looked down the hole.

It was dark and apparently endless.

Tim shuffled along one side of the hole. Grk went round the other. They were just about to keep running when, up ahead, they saw one of the men coming towards them.

He was smiling.

Tim looked back and saw why.

There was the other man, the other brother, the other twin, running towards them. His gun was raised. But he didn't bother firing. There was no need. Tim was trapped between them. He couldn't run either way without smacking straight into one of them.

Tim had a simple choice.

He could surrender.

Or he could jump down the hole.

If he surrendered they would probably shoot him and drop his body down the hole.

If he jumped down the hole himself he'd probably break every bone in his body.

Which was worse?

Grk was turning his head from side to side, looking first at one of the brothers, then the other, as if he was deciding which of them to fight first.

Grk was a brave dog, Tim knew that, but he wasn't particularly sensible. And he didn't know much about guns or criminals. He didn't realise that a boy and a dog didn't stand a a chance against two big men with pistols.

The men were closer now. They'd slowed to a walking pace. There was no need to keep running. Alberto smiled at his brother, and Antonio smiled back.

Under his breath Tim hissed, 'Jump!'

Grk looked up at him and wagged his tail. He could

understand that Tim was playing another game, but he wasn't sure of the rules.

'Jump,' said Tim again, speaking a little louder this time.

Grk wagged his tail even more, but he still didn't move.

Tim glanced at the brothers, who were now advancing on him, their guns drawn. If he didn't jump down the hole, they'd probably push him. But if he jumped he might avoid getting shot first. In one swift movement he gathered Grk in his arms and jumped down the hole.

Behind him, above him, he heard the sounds of two men shouting. There was a bang, then another. Then all other sounds were swept away by the extraordinary sensation of dropping through the air, plunging down the deep, dark tunnel of the black hole.

Air raced over his face. His hair stood up on end.

Wwwwooooooaaaaahhh! howled Grk.

Tim closed his eyes and waited for the terrible pain that he knew would be waiting for him at the bottom of the hole.

Alberto and Antonio stood over the hole and looked down, down, down into the dark depths.

Alberto pointed his gun into the darkness and fired a shot.

Antonio did the same.

Then they waited.

But not a sound came back.

Not a scream. Not a shout. Not even a thump or a bump or a bang as their bullets smacked into the dirt at the bottom of the hole.

The only sound was silence.

Alberto looked at Antonio, then nodded at the hole. 'You wanna jump down there after him?'

'No thanks,' said Antonio. 'How about you?'

'Not me,' said Alberto.

They both shuffled forward and peered down the dark pit again.

It was impossible to see the bottom. Anything might have been down there. For all they knew the hole carried on for hundreds of metres, plunging into the very centre of the earth.

'He couldn't have survived a drop like that,' said Antonio. 'Could he?'

'Not a chance,' Alberto confirmed. 'Even if he did, he's never gonna get out of there. He musta broke his legs.'

'Maybe his skull too,' said Antonio.

'Definitely his skull too,' agreed Alberto. 'He's dead already.'

'If he ain't, the monster will soon get him.'

'The monster!' said Alberto, smiling for the first time in a long while. 'You don't believe all those stupid stories, do you?'

'Sure I do,' said Antonio. 'I even heard it once.'

'You heard the monster?'

'Sure I did.'

'You never told me that before. When was it? What happened?'

'I dunno. A year ago, maybe two. I was in the cellar, fetching a bottle for the duke, and I heard it screaming.

I gotta tell you, bro, that was a bad sound. I wouldn't want to find myself down a deep, dark hole with that monster. He sounded angry. And hungry too. So you don't have to worry about that dumb kid and his dumb dog. If they ain't dead already, they will be soon.'

Chapter Thirty-One

Opposite the Palazzo Macaroni there was a small, smart café, predictably named the Café Macaroni. It had nothing to do with the duke, and he had never even stepped through the doorway, but the café's owners had borrowed the name from the famous family who lived across the street.

It was late, but the café was still open. There was an empty table by the window. Alessandra sat there, ordered an orange juice from the waiter and stared at the Palazzo Macaroni. What was happening behind those walls? Was Tim safe? Had he found Grk? Or had he been seen and caught by *il Duca*'s armed guards?

She reached into her pocket and pulled out her phone. She'd put it on silent earlier in the day. Now she saw that she had twenty-seven missed calls, all from the same person. Her father. She rang him back.

When he answered, she could hear the panic in his voice.

'*Ciao, Papà,*' she said.

Before she could say another word Salvatore Pecorino bombarded her with questions, demanding to know where she had been for the past two hours and what she was doing right now.

'Don't worry, Papa,' said Alessandra, explaining that she just had delivered Tim to the centre of the city.

'You didn't say you were going to do that! You said you were going to put him in a taxi!'

'I thought you wouldn't mind. You were so busy with your mozzarella.'

'Don't be silly, Alessandra. You're only a child. I didn't know where you were. Anything might have happened! I've been going out of my mind with panic. Where are you now?'

'I told you, Papa. In the city.'

'Where in the city?'

'In a café.'

'Which café? Where is it? I want to come and find you.'

'Don't worry, Papa. I can look after myself.'

'Tell me where you are.'

'Papa—'

'Just tell me where you are.'

Alessandra sighed. She could have put the phone down, or told a lie, but she couldn't treat her father like that. He'd always been honest with her, and so she was honest back again. She gave the address of the café opposite the Palazzo Macaroni.

'I will see you very soon,' said Salvatore Pecorino.

'Yes, Papa,' said Alessandra.

'Don't move.'

'No, Papa.'

'*Ciao,* Alessandra.'

'*Ciao, Papà.*'

She ended the call, took another sip of her orange juice and stared at the big steel gates, hoping Tim and Grk would emerge before her father arrived.

Chapter Thirty-Two

Something was licking Tim's face.

Something warm. And wet.

Something with very bad breath.

He opened his eyes and said, 'Hello, Grk.'

Grk responded by covering his face with even more slobber.

'Urgh, don't do that,' Tim gasped. He rolled over and sat up. Then he groaned.

Everything hurt.

His back, his legs, his knees, his elbows, his head – they all hurt.

He wondered how long he had been lying here. Minutes? Hours? He didn't know, and he had no way of telling.

He remembered what had just happened to him. He'd been falling down that black hole when he hit the side. He bounced and hit the other side, then bounced again. The hole narrowed, which must have slowed him down, and he was rattled back and forth like one of those silver balls in a pinball machine, before finally dropping down again and smacking onto the ground. That was when the world went black.

He must have been knocked out. Now he was awake again and he rather wished he wasn't. When you're unconscious, nothing hurts.

In the darkness he couldn't even see Grk, but he could tell that the little dog was fine, because he could hear him prancing back and forth, yapping eagerly, trying to persuade Tim to get up and start moving.

'*Shh!*' hissed Tim.

Grk shushed.

Tim listened to the silence.

He couldn't hear anything. No voices, no footsteps, no bullets. Either the two men were listening out for him, keeping very quiet, or, more likely, they'd decided he was dead, and gone away.

Even if he wasn't dead, they had probably said to one another, he would be trapped down here for the last remaining hours of his life. Without food. Without water. Lost and lonely and unable to see anything, even his own hands in front of his face. Counting out his last remaining hours till he starved to death.

Perhaps they were right.

Or perhaps there was another way out, an exit that they didn't know about.

But how was he going to find it?

Which way should he go?

If only he had a torch he could explore more of the cellar.

He didn't need a torch, he decided. He could find his way by touch.

He would also be guided by Grk. Dogs have better night vision than humans, so Grk should be able to see his way around down here. As long as they stayed close to one another, Grk should be able to lead him safely through the cellars.

He eased himself to his feet, gasping as he realised just how much his body hurt.

He checked himself all over. He'd smashed his kneecaps and bashed his elbows and bruised his head and thumped his toes and crumpled his fingers, but nothing actually appeared to be broken. He was still in full working order.

The thick dust was tickling Tim's throat and he could have done with a drink to wash it away. Maybe he'd find some water in another part of the cellar. He wouldn't be at all surprised if an underground stream ran through these caverns.

Suddenly Grk growled.

'What is it?' whispered Tim.

Grk growled again.

Tim peered into the darkness, wondering what Grk could sense. Had those two men come back again? Were they about to jump out and attack him? What if they had torches? He wouldn't be able to defend himself. There was no point putting up his hands and trying to surrender. They'd just shoot him. So what should he do? Hide? Run? Or...?

Then he heard it too.

There was a noise coming from deeper in the cellar. A strange, shuffling, scuffling noise. As if someone – or something – was moving slowly towards him.

It couldn't be the twins. They wouldn't shuffle or scuffle.

So what was it?

Unable to see anything in the gloom, Tim found his imagination conjuring up horrible possibilities. There might be any kind of beast down in these cellars, kept here by the duke to eat his prisoners. It might be a big dog. A wolf. A bear. Or even a ghost.

Don't be ridiculous, Tim told himself. Ghosts don't exist.

Grk was growling constantly now. His ears were upright and his tail was down.

Tim crouched and placed his hand on Grk's back. 'Shh,' he whispered. 'Shhhh.'

Reluctantly, Grk stopped growling.

They waited together in silence.

They didn't have to wait long. The shuffling grew louder and a shape soon emerged from the gloom.

It was a man.

A small man.

With a long straggly beard hanging halfway down his front. His feet were bare and his clothes were baggy. In his right hand, the man was carrying a stub of candle, dribbling wax onto his fingers.

Whoever he was, he looked – and smelled – as if he'd been living in the cellar for several years. He hadn't bathed, shaved or changed his clothes for a very long time.

He didn't appear to have noticed Tim. He was hobbling past, staring straight ahead. If Tim stayed very still, the man would be gone in a moment, taking his candle, his smell and his beard deeper into the darkness.

Unfortunately Grk chose that moment to start barking.

Tim knelt down and put his hands on the dog's neck. '*Shh!*' he hissed. '*Shhhhhhhh!*'

But Grk took no notice. He just barked more loudly and more fiercely, warning this stranger, this intruder, of his presence. *Get out,* Grk was saying. *Go away. We're here and we want to be left alone.*

The man turned towards them.

He blinked and stared, peering into the gloom.

Then he shuffled forward, holding the candle at the end of his outstretched arm.

In the light Tim could see the man's face. He had wild staring eyes and long tangled hair.

His mouth opened and a voice emerged.

It was a crackly voice – a voice that sounded as if it didn't get used very often – and it spoke Italian.

Grk barked again, even more loudly, telling this wild man to keep his distance.

Tim didn't know what to do or what to say. Should he dodge towards the stranger and try to knock the candle from his hand? That might work. In the confusion and the darkness he might be able to get away, running down a corridor before the madman caught him.

Yes, he thought. That's what I should do. He took a deep breath, trying to calm his beating heart, and was just about to hurl himself forward when the wild man knelt on the ground and reached out with his right hand. His palm was flat. His fingers were open. In his croaky voice, he said, '*Buona sera, cucciolo. Come sta?*'

Grk didn't answer. Of course he didn't. He couldn't speak. But he did sniff the man's hand.

Tim wanted to call him back and say, 'Don't be stupid, he's a wild man with wild hair and wild staring eyes, you mustn't go anywhere near him.'

But Grk must have decided that the wild man didn't actually smell too bad because he allowed his ears to be tickled. He didn't even protest or run away when the man shuffled forward and stroked his back.

The wild man caressed Grk for a minute or two. Then he looked up at Tim and said, '*Ciao, ragazzo. Cosa fai qui?*'

'I don't know what you're saying,' Tim told him. 'I can't speak Italian.'

'You are English?' asked the man with a strong accent.

'Yes. Do you speak English?'

'Once upon a time, yes I did, but that was very many years ago.' The wild man smiled, showing two rows of crooked, blackened, rotten teeth. 'But I don't speak very much of the Italian neither, these days. So English just as good.'

'Who are you?' asked Tim.

'My name is Massimo Mascarpone,' said the wild man. 'And I am the thirteenth Duke of Macaroni.'

Chapter Thirty-Three

'Alessandra? Alessandra?'

Alessandra turned her head and saw her father. She hadn't noticed him coming into the café. She had hardly even heard his voice until he leaned across the table and took her arm. She smiled and said, '*Ciao, Papà.*'

'*Ciao.* Where is Tim?'

'His parents came to collect him. They took him back to their hotel.'

'Leaving you here? All alone?'

'They knew you were coming to collect me.'

Salvatore was surprised, but he didn't say anything. He didn't like criticising other people, especially if he'd never even met them. 'It is very late. You should be in bed too, Alessandra. We've got another busy day tomorrow. Come on, let's go.'

As they emerged from the café, Alessandra glanced across the street at the big steel gates of the Palazzo Macaroni.

Nothing had changed. The gates were still firmly shut. The guards were standing under the streetlights, laughing and chatting. A few teenagers were kicking a football against the palazzo's wall and a couple of tourists had stopped to take a picture, but there was no sign of an English boy or the silver Mercedes which had taken him inside.

Alessandra thought about Tim. She had given him her phone number and the name of the hotel where they were staying, and told him to ring or turn up at any time of day or night. She hoped he was safe. She hoped he hadn't been caught by the duke or his thugs. She hoped—

'Come on, Alessandra,' said Salvatore. 'This is not the moment for daydreaming. It's very late and you haven't even had supper yet.'

'Sorry, Papa.' Alessandra turned her back on the Palazzo Macaroni and followed her father down the street.

In the huge hallway of the Palazzo Macaroni the Duchess of Macaroni was giving orders to her servants, sending each of them in a different direction.

The Palazzo Macaroni had about a hundred rooms and a huge garden. Peppi might have hidden himself anywhere, but she wasn't going to give up until she found him.

She ordered her servants to comb every centimetre of the house and gardens. Peppi couldn't have climbed the walls or sneaked out through the gate. He must be here somewhere. She wanted them to find him – and she would give a thousand euros to whoever did.

'Now, my darling,' said the duke, when his wife had finished giving her orders to the servants, 'shouldn't you be in bed?'

'Bed? *Bed?* How can I go to bed at a time like this?'

'You don't have to be here. The staff can search for Peppi without you.'

'Don't be ridiculous,' the duchess snapped. 'I want to search with them.'

'But, my sweet, you're going to be on television tomorrow morning. The whole country will see you watching my speech. You want to look your best, don't you?'

'If I haven't found Peppi, I won't be there.'

'What do you mean? You have to be there!'

'If you're so keen for me to hear your speech,' snapped the duchess, 'you shouldn't have let your stupid bodyguards walk off with Peppi. He hasn't been the same since.'

'I'm so sorry, darling,' said the duke, looking around for his two bodyguards. He couldn't see Alberto or Antonio. Where were they? Why weren't they helping his wife? Had they already gone to bed? He thought not. They preferred late nights. But he was glad they weren't here. If his wife started quizzing them about the details of their day with 'Peppi' they were sure to get themselves in a terrible muddle, and she'd grow even more suspicious. 'I promise you, my sweet, they won't be allowed to go anywhere near your dog ever again.'

The duchess didn't hear him. She was already marching down the hallway, her high heels clacking on the polished marble floor, joining the search for Peppi.

The duke stared after her and sighed.

Dogs, he thought. Why were they so determined to ruin his life?

It didn't matter, he told himself. He didn't need to worry about Peppi or his wife. He had more important things to think about. His speech, for instance. And the elections. And all the Italian people who wanted to vote for him.

Trying to forget his wife, he walked upstairs to his bedroom, determined to get a good night's sleep. He wanted to look his best for all the cameras tomorrow.

Chapter Thirty-Four

Massimo led Tim and Grk through the catacombs to a large cave.

'*Ecco, la mia casa*,' he said. 'Here is my home.'

Tim looked around the cave, which was lit by a couple of flickering candles. He thought about his own home – his bedroom, the kitchen, the big, comfy sofa where he sat and played computer games – and felt very glad that he didn't live in a cold, dark cave.

Massimo gave them a quick tour, proudly showing them the bed, chair and shelves that he had made from old wine crates, and pointing out the hole in the roof that provided sunlight during the day.

'You are hungry?' he asked.

'I'd love a drink,' said Tim. 'I'm sure Grk would too.'

Massimo fetched water for them both.

Grk lapped his from a saucer, and chomped on a little lump of cheese. Then he walked three times in a circle and lay down. For the first time since that morning, when he had been chasing squirrels in Hyde Park, he was happy.

Massimo told Tim to sit on a crate, then fetched an old shirt and ripped it apart.

Tim winced as Massimo tightened the home-made bandage around his knee.

'That does hurt?' asked Massimo.

'No,' lied Tim, trying to be brave. 'It's fine.'

'Then I will do one more leg.' Massimo tore off a second strip of cloth and wrapped it around Tim's other knee.

As Massimo tended to Tim's wounds, he told him how he came to be living down here in the catacombs.

Eighteen years ago, he said, he had been walking through the Palazzo Macaroni with his twin brother, Giovanni. They had been born within a few minutes of one another. Now they were discussing their father, who was just about to die.

They should choose a wonderful bottle of wine, Giovanni suggested, and give their father a final drink. He should be allowed to enjoy his last hours on earth washing down his medicine with a good prosecco or a delicious glass of Barolo rather than water.

It was a good idea, Massimo thought. He was impressed. His younger brother wasn't usually so thoughtful. Perhaps Giovanni had been changed by their father's illness. Perhaps he would now stop behaving like such a fool and start acting like a true Macaroni.

Together, the Macaroni twins went down to the cellars to choose a bottle of wine.

They didn't tell anyone where they were going. They wanted it to be a surprise for their father. They would pick the best wine in the cellars and take it up to his bedroom.

They walked through the dark corridors, Giovanni leading the way. Massimo wasn't sure where they were going; he rarely came down to these cellars. But his brother swore that he knew exactly where to find the perfect bottle.

'It's this way,' said Giovanni. 'Up ahead, there's a secret cellar that almost no one knows about. Papa took me there last year. Here we are, yes, at the end of this corridor. You go ahead. I'll light the way with the torch.'

Massimo did as he was told. He walked along the corridor, looking left and right, searching for the entrance to the cellar.

Midway down the corridor he came to a hole in the floor. He looked into it. The hole seemed to go on for ever. He said, 'Look, Giovanni. Look at this. I wonder what it is.'

'A hole,' said his brother, standing behind him.

'I can see that. But I wonder where it goes.'

'There's only one way to find out. You should jump down it.'

Massimo laughed. 'I don't think that's a good idea.'

'I think it is,' said his brother. 'In fact, I think you should do it right now.'

Massimo laughed again and turned round. His smile faded when he saw what his brother was holding.

'What's that?' he asked.

'What does it look like?'

'A gun.'

'That's right,' said Giovanni. 'It is a gun.'

'Why are you pointing it at me? Are you going to kill me?'

'Of course not. Do you think I'm a monster? I couldn't murder my own brother. Killing you would be like killing myself, Massimo, and I don't want to do that. No, my dear brother, I just want to get rid of you for a little while. A week, perhaps. Maybe two. No longer. Then you can come out again. Now, jump!'

'What do you mean, "get rid of me"?'

'I mean exactly what I said. I want you to go away for some time. When Papa dies I want to be the only Macaroni left here. Now, please, stop asking so many questions and jump. Or I really will have to shoot you.'

Massimo could see the madness in his brother's eyes. He realised he didn't have any choice. If he didn't jump he would be shot.

So he jumped.

The hole seemed to go on for ever, dropping him down into the darkest depths of the earth.

He had been here ever since.

At the beginning he'd really believed that his brother was just going to leave him down here for a week or two. But a fortnight passed. Then another. And Massimo was still stuck in the darkness, unable to return to his home, to his old life.

Every few days Giovanni lowered a basket of provisions down the hole on a long rope.

Sometimes the basket would contain more than just food and water. Giovanni might send candles, a box of matches, a pack of cards or a bottle of wine. He dropped down books too and even an occasional newspaper.

Reading one of those newspapers, Massimo learnt of his father's death. Reading another, he discovered what the world believed had happened to him. A pile of his clothes had been found on the beach at Rapallo, a beautiful resort where the Macaroni family owned a summer house. A note had been found in the pocket of his trousers, written in his handwriting, saying that he was tired of life. According to the newspaper the present Duke of Macaroni, Giovanni Mascarpone, believed his brother had been grief-stricken at their father's death.

When he read that, Massimo understood why he was in the hole. His brother was determined to inherit the family title and wouldn't let anything – or anyone – stand in his way.

That was when Massimo understood that he was going to be down there for the rest of his life.

He understood why his brother hadn't murdered him. They were twins. They had known one another for their entire lives. And they looked exactly alike. For Massimo, killing Giovanni really would be like killing himself, and Giovanni must have felt exactly the same way.

But even if Giovanni wasn't going to kill him, he would never let him go.

If he was going to live down here, Massimo realised, he had better find himself a decent cave. He explored the entire catacombs and chose one with a tiny chink in the roof which let in some natural light.

This was where he had brought Tim and Grk, and this was where they were sitting now.

Tim looked around at the murky cave, then at Grk, who was dozing happily on the ground.

Tim wished he felt happy too. But he didn't. He felt angry and bitter and impatient and trapped. He wanted to tell his parents where he was and stop them worrying. He wanted to tell the world what had happened to the real Duke of Macaroni. He wanted to ask Giovanni Mascarpone why he had mistreated his twin brother so horribly. But he couldn't do any of these things unless he found a way to get out of the catacombs. So what he could do? How was he going to escape from here?

Would this be his home for the next eighteen years, just as it had been Massimo's? Would he have to stay down here till he died? Would he never see his own bedroom again?

He thought about Max and Natascha. Would they be panicking? Or talking to the police? Or trying to track down him and Grk?

He should have rung them when he had a chance. Even if they couldn't have helped him, at least he could have said goodbye.

Rung them, he thought.

Yes!

That's exactly what he should have done. Why hadn't he thought of it before?

He pulled something from his pocket.

'This will get us out of here,' he said.

Massimo stared at the small, thin, black object. 'What is that?'

'You've never seen one of these before?'

'Never,' said Massimo.

'That's because you've been stuck in a cellar for eighteen years. While you've been down here the world has changed. This is called a mobile phone.'

'This is *un telefono?*'

'That's what I said; a phone.'

'*Ma, non è possibile!* I mean, this is not possible, to have *uno telefono* so small.'

'It must be possible,' said Tim. 'Because I'm holding it.'

'You can call someone? On this?'

'Yes.'

'But how?'

'I don't know how it works, but it works. We just have to find somewhere with reception.'

'"*Reception*"? What is this *reception*?'

Tim explained as well as he could.

Massimo nodded. 'I will take you through the catacombs,' he said. 'We will find a place for your *reception*. First, how are your legs? You can stand up? Here, let me help you.'

'No, I'm fine,' said Tim. And he was. His legs supported his weight without any problem. Falling down the hole had battered and bruised him, covering his body with nicks and scratches, but he wasn't seriously damaged. He felt fine, in fact.

'Come on, Grk,' he said. 'Time to wake up. Let's get out of here.'

Grk sprang to his feet and barked excitedly.

Massimo led them through the dark and gloomy catacombs, searching for a spot that offered good reception.

As they walked Tim stared at the phone in his right hand, pressing the keys every few moments to light up the display.

A line of five bars marked the level of reception. There was never more than one lit up, and that wasn't enough to make a call.

They walked the length and breadth of Massimo's prison, pacing the caves and corridors, but couldn't find anywhere with good enough reception for Tim to make a phone call.

Tim's shoulders slumped. His brilliant plan wasn't so brilliant after all. Without reception, his phone was just a useless lump of shiny metal. 'What am I going to do?' he said, more to himself than to Massimo.

'There is one other chance to get away,' the Italian said.

'Oh, yes? What is it?'

'You are smaller than me, no?' asked Massimo.

'Much smaller.'

'And also thinner?'

'Yes.'

'Then I have an idea. For many years I have been planning my escape. With this.'

Massimo reached into his pocket and pulled out something which looked like a teaspoon.

Leaning forward to get a better look, Tim realised that it *was* a teaspoon.

'You're going to escape from the catacombs with a spoon?' he said.

'*Si!*' said Massimo.

'But how?'

'Come with me and I will show you.'

Chapter Thirty-Five

Two thousand years ago, Massimo explained, when Rome was ruled by the Romans, these catacombs had offered a hiding place for escaped prisoners. The first Christians had taken refuge here. So had gladiators who managed to break their bonds and flee from the Colosseum before the day of their final fight.

The Romans would not follow anyone into the catacombs. They would simply post a guard outside. He would stand there, armed with a sword and a shield, waiting for the hungry, thirsty, bleary-eyed prisoners to stumble out of the darkness and beg for food and water.

Some of the prisoners refused to surrender. Twenty centuries later, their skeletons were still there.

During the years that Massimo had been stuck down in the catacombs he had explored every cave, every passageway, every corridor, searching for a way to get out. He'd found a few holes in the rock. Most of them were high in the roofs of big caves, impossible to reach without a rope or a ladder. He'd also discovered an entrance to the catacombs. This was the entrance, he thought, that those prisoners had used two thousand years ago.

At some point since then, this entrance had been blocked up. Now Massimo was trying to unblock it again.

Every day he had been chipping away at the rock with his teaspoon.

It was slow work.

Very slow work.

But he was making progress. Day by day, week by week, month by month, year by year, the hole had been getting bigger.

He had now been working on it for seven years, but he still hadn't managed to make a hole which was big enough for himself. He had been planning to carry on scraping the rock for another three or four years. Then he might be able to squeeze through.

But the hole was already big enough for a dog.

And probably for a boy too.

Massimo led Tim and Grk through the catacombs to a small cave, lit by a tiny chink of sunlight in the top corner. It was dawn. Above them, the city would be waking up. The streets would be full of people going to work and kids going to school. Tim wanted to be among them, not stuck down here in the dark.

He turned to Massimo. 'If I get out through here, what about you? What will you do?'

Massimo shrugged his shoulders. 'I will be here for another three or four years. Is no problem. After eighteen years, three or four more is no problem.'

'I'll bring a digger and smash a hole into the catacombs.'

'You will drive a digger into the Palazzo Macaroni? I don't think so.'

'Then I'll tell the police. They'll come and get you.'

'I have a better idea,' said Massimo. 'You can go to Santa Maria dei Gemelli.'

'Who's she?'

Massimo smiled. 'She is not a woman, my friend. She is a place. Across the street from the Palazzo Macaroni there is a beautiful church with the name Santa Maria dei Gemelli. I have been there very many times as a boy. In the crypt of the church, down in the cellar, there is a well, a deep hole in the floor. This hole comes here to the catacombs. Many times, Tim, I have shouted up that hole, hoping the priest will hear me, but he never does. If you can go there with a rope, and it is long enough, you can fetch me out.'

So it was decided: when Tim got out of the Palazzo Macaroni he would find a rope and go to the church of Santa Maria dei Gemelli, where Massimo would be waiting far below him.

But first Tim had to get out of the catacombs.

To reach the hole they had to clamber up a rough staircase, which had been carved out of the rock, probably by the same prisoners or gladiators who had sheltered in these caves two thousand years ago.

At the top of the staircase, they came to a wall built of cement, stones and rubble. Part of this wall had been made by the Romans, said Massimo, and part had been added recently by the Dukes of Macaroni, sealing up these catacombs to keep them safe.

In the middle of the wall there was a narrow hole.

This was the hole that Massimo had made with his spoon.

Tim lifted Grk up and pushed him through the hole.

Grk wasn't very pleased about it, but he didn't have

much choice. He scrambled through, jumped down the other side and yapped a few times, demanding to know what was going on.

'Don't worry!' Tim called through the hole. 'I'll be with you soon.'

He took off his shoes, his socks, his shirt and his trousers, making himself as slim as possible. Then he clambered up the rock and tried to squeeze himself through the hole.

He was too big.

The hole was too small.

He could feel the rock squeezing him.

Squishing his bones. Scraping his skin.

He pulled himself forward with his arms.

Massimo pushed his feet.

Up ahead, Tim could see daylight. He could hear Grk barking excitedly, willing him to move faster. He wriggled and jiggled, pulling himself with his hands while Massimo continued pushing him from behind.

He was stuck.

He couldn't move forward or backwards.

He would have to stay here for ever.

He pulled himself towards the light. The rock scraped his skin, but he tried to ignore the pain. A little further, he told himself. Just a little further and he'd be out of there.

His head emerged.

Immediately Grk jumped up and licked his face.

Tim giggled and pushed him away. He pulled himself again.

Finally he popped out, squeezed like toothpaste from a tube, and rolled onto the ground.

He stood up and looked around. He appeared to be in a ditch in the garden of the Palazzo Macaroni. Above him there was a metal grille. He pushed it. The grille lifted. He would be able to get out.

Massimo was already pushing his clothes through the hole.

'Careful of the phone,' said Tim. 'Don't drop it on the—'

But he was too late. His mobile dropped straight onto the stone, followed by his clothes and shoes.

Tim picked up the phone. The screen was cracked. He tried to switch it on, but nothing happened. It was dead.

He'd been planning to call Alessandra, the police or his parents – if not all three – and ask them to get him out of here.

He couldn't do that. He couldn't call anyone.

He might have escaped from the catacombs, but he was still trapped in the Palazzo Macaroni, the wrong side of a high wall and some big steel gates. How was he going to get out of here?

Chapter Thirty-Six

Even at this early hour of the morning a couple of gardeners were walking slowly along the gravel paths, watering plants. They chatted in low voices, discussing the latest striker who had signed for Lazio, their beloved football team. He had cost forty million euros, but he hadn't scored a single goal all season. What was wrong with him? Had they been cheated? Were the referees biased against them? Or was he just an idiot who spent too much time in nightclubs rather than practising his free kicks?

They were so absorbed in their dissection of the striker's failures that they didn't notice a boy and a dog sneaking through the bushes behind them.

Tim jogged down the gravel path, watching out for any more gardeners. Grk sprinted alongside him, delighted to be outside at last after all those hours cooped up in the catacombs.

They soon came to a large windowless building with an open door. Tim would have walked straight past, but Grk nipped inside.

'Hey!' hissed Tim. 'Come back here!'

But Grk didn't.

Sighing, Tim hurried after him. Why would Grk never do what he was told? Why did he always want to go exploring? Hadn't he learnt anything from his recent experiences?

Inside the big building Grk was having a pee against the wheel of an enormous red Rolls Royce with leather seats and silver fittings. It looked like the type of car that cost a million dollars, and probably was.

The Rolls Royce was parked in a long line of shiny vehicles of all shapes and sizes. There were limousines and sports cars, jeeps and motorbikes, Ferraris and Maseratis, Alfa Romeos and Harley-Davidsons.

This must be the duke's collection, Tim realised. These were his cars and his bikes. Whatever he wanted to drive, however he fancied travelling, he could come down here and pick the perfect ride.

And now Tim could do the same.

On the wall beside the door thirty hooks held thirty keys, tempting him to pick one and drive off.

He looked around the garage, trying to decide what to borrow for his great escape.

His eyes lingered on a gleaming red Ferrari. If he took that he could drive so fast that the duke's guards would never catch him.

Of course, he'd have to start the car first. And point it in the right direction. And get out of those big steel gates.

No, a sports car was too big for him. He'd rather drive something smaller and more manoeuvrable.

Like one of those mopeds parked at the end of the garage, for instance. One of those nippy, zippy little mopeds. They would be perfect.

Tim had been on a bike like this once before – in Rio de Janeiro, in Brazil. Then he'd been riding on the back, clinging onto the shirt of a boy named Zito, while Grk tucked himself between them. This was different. This time Tim would have to ride it himself.

And start it himself.

In Brazil Zito had jump-started the moped by sticking a knife into the ignition. Tim didn't have to do anything so tricky. He could use a key. He hurried over to the hooks and grabbed all the keys, gathering them up with both hands.

Along the wall beside the keys there were several shelves crammed with motoring accessories. Even the most pernickety driver would find what he wanted here. There were scarves and caps, spanners and hammers, spare windscreen wipers and tins of oil. There were leather gloves of all shapes, sizes and colours. And there were at least thirty helmets, some large, some small, and one tiny enough for a dog. Tim grabbed that one, then tried a couple of others himself. When he found one that fitted, he put it on his head and clipped the strap under his chin. Then he sat on the moped and tried the keys in the ignition one at a time.

When he found the right key he dumped the others on the floor and turned it in the ignition.

Nothing happened.

Why not? What was he doing wrong?

He tried to remember how Zito had started and ridden the moped. Ah, yes. That's right. You don't just turn the key. You have to twist the throttle at the same time.

Trying to replicate exactly what Zito had done, Tim twisted the throttle and turned the key again.

This time the engine coughed into life. Tim turned the throttle a little further and the moped lurched forward, almost throwing him off. He managed to cling on, and chugged around the garage, steering an unsteady course between a Ferrari and an Alfa Romeo.

He giggled. This was fun. Riding a moped didn't feel so different to riding a bicycle. Just a bit faster. He did a couple of turns, keeping his balance better each time, then shouted to Grk: 'Jump on!'

Grk put his head to one side and stared quizzically at Tim as if to say: *Are you serious?*

'It's perfectly safe,' insisted Tim, slapping the front of his leather seat. 'Come up here!'

Grk sniffed the air a couple of times, like he was checking out the moped, but didn't move. He obviously wasn't convinced.

'Here!' said Tim, slapping the front of his leather seat. 'Here, Grk! Here!'

If Grk was human he would have shaken his head. But he was a dog, so he answered in his own doggy way: he turned his back on Tim and wandered over to the rear wheel of a silver Lexus, where he lifted his leg and had another pee.

Fine, thought Tim. Stay here if you want. I'll go and save the world on my own.

He didn't say any of that aloud. Riding a moped was tough enough; he didn't want to talk too.

Also, he didn't really mean it. He wasn't going to leave Grk behind. Of course he wasn't. He'd already been knocked out, tied up, stuffed in a crate and dropped down a hole while he was trying to save this aggravating dog. Now he'd saved him, he wasn't going to abandon him. He revved the throttle. The bike sprang forward. He turned the handlebars and raced around the garage once again, moving faster this time and bumping into a couple of cars, leaving a long scratch down the length of a Maserati and cracking the wing mirror of a silver Lamborghini.

Ignoring the damage that he'd just caused, he turned another corner and drove along the back wall of the garage. Up ahead he could see Grk. Tim headed straight for him. Holding the handlebars with one hand, he reached down to the ground with his other and scooped up Grk.

Woah! yelped Grk, taken entirely by surprise.

At the front of all mopeds, just behind the handlebars, there is a little ledge where smart Italians put their shoes and their shopping bags. That was where Tim put Grk.

Woof! complained Grk, who didn't like to be treated like a shoe or a shopping bag.

Tim took no notice. He knew Grk wouldn't jump off. Not when they were whizzing along, anyway. He turned to the right and chugged through the open door. Just before they shot out of the garage he popped the spare helmet on Grk's head. It fitted perfectly.

The gardeners had gone. There was no one to be seen. Tim drove slowly and carefully down the path. Gravel spat under the moped's wheels. Soon he came to a line of trees from where he could see the big steel gates which were keeping him in here.

The gates were shut.

What could he do?

He knew already that there wasn't another way out of the palazzo.

He couldn't drive through the gates. Nor could he jump over them. Not even on this moped.

Had he chosen the wrong vehicle? Should he go back and try to steal a truck or a limousine instead?

He looked down. Grk was preparing to leap from the moped. He wanted to go exploring.

'Stay,' said Tim.

Grk looked up at him as if to say: *Why?*

Tim was just about to answer when he noticed that the gates had started to move.

They were opening.

Through the gap in the gates Tim could see the street outside, and some guards, and a big black van with tinted windows.

One of the guards was speaking into his walkie-talkie. Another was scratching his nose. Two more were sharing a joke, chuckling and nodding their heads.

Tim turned the throttle.

The moped sprang forward.

Two of the guards were blocking Tim's way now. He couldn't swerve round them, so he went straight for them, hoping they'd get out of his path.

Grrrr! growled Grk, preparing himself to launch an attack on these two enemies he'd spotted up ahead.

One of the guards heard the sound of the engine and looked up. He shouted a warning to his companion and they both leaped aside.

Tim roared straight through the space where the two guards had just been standing.

He sped through the gates.

A guard yelled into his walkie-talkie. Another pressed an alarm button. The others started running, reaching into their holsters and pulling out pistols.

They didn't know who had just sped past them. Under his helmet, they couldn't see his face. He might have been a thief who'd stolen the duchess's diamonds, a terrorist who'd planted a bomb, or an assassin who was plotting to murder their boss. But they knew they had to stop him.

Moments after the moped and its rider had gone through the gates a small army of men and cars headed into the streets of Rome, determined to catch him, whoever he was.

Chapter Thirty-Seven

The moped danced under him. The wheels slithered on the road. The body swayed back and forth. Tim clung to the handlebars and fought to keep control.

He knew he was being chased, but he couldn't turn his head to see who was behind him. If he did, he'd fall off.

He turned the throttle to maximum and sped through the streets, hoping he wouldn't hit anyone or anything.

Down at Tim's feet Grk skidded from side to side, the wind flapping his tail and skimming over his fur.

Their moped ploughed through the middle of a café, scattering customers who had been calmly eating their breakfast. A waiter was thrown aside. His tray went flying. Coffee cups and teaspoons rained down on the ground.

Tim heard shouts and screams. He saw people jumping out of the way. He would have liked to stop and say sorry, but he knew he couldn't. He just had to get out of here as fast as he could.

He drove down a cobbled street. The moped bounced around like a bucking horse trying to throw him off. He held on tight with both hands. Grk swung from side to side, scrabbling with his paws, trying to stay aboard.

He sped past an artist who had got up early to paint the Forum. The moped knocked his easel, the canvas fell to the floor and landed facedown, and the painter put his head in his hands. All his hard work was ruined!

Tim clipped a market stall. Peaches and melons bounced along the road. The stallholder waved his fist and shouted a stream of curses.

Tim dodged round him and sped into the middle of the road.

Two cars swerved to avoid him and slammed together. Metal crunched and glass tinkled.

Trying to miss a third car, Tim executed a quick turn and found himself on the wrong side of the road.

Cars were driving towards him.

He steered by them, desperately trying to keep his balance.

A lorry swept past with a great gush of wind, almost toppling him from his bike.

A bus hooted.

A policeman waved his arms and blew his whistle.

Tim sped down the middle of the road, swerving round them all.

One by one the Duke of Macaroni's guards crashed, smashed, bashed and destroyed their cars, until only four of them were still in the chase; four men on motorbikes, roaring through the traffic, keeping pace with the midget on the moped.

They bumped down a flight of stairs after him, zoomed up a highway on the wrong side of the road and wiggled through the traffic.

Tim never saw them. He didn't dare look back. He

just kept his hand on the throttle and his eyes on the road, watching what was coming towards him.

Up ahead he could see a huge monument. He didn't know what it was, although he was sure that he'd seen it somewhere before. He saw a crowd of tourists and a line of bollards and a pavement and an ice-cream salesman setting up his stall, preparing for a busy day ahead.

And then he saw a line of gladiators.

A line of *gladiators*?

For a moment Tim thought his eyes must be playing tricks on him, and then he realised that, somehow, these twenty men really did appear to be gladiators. They were wearing long red smocks and silver armour. They were carrying shields, swords and spears, and their heads were protected by heavy helmets. They looked as if they were waiting to fight a lion or hoping for a thumbs up from the emperor.

That moment – the moment Tim spent working out that, yes, he really was driving at high speed towards twenty Roman gladiators – was the moment that he messed up. He was going too fast to waste time thinking. He had to swerve or he was going to run straight into them. He yanked the handlebars to the left. The wheels screeched. Grk yelped. Tim soared into the air. His moped flipped over.

With a smash and a crash and a groan of crushed metal, the front of the moped rammed straight into the ice-cream cart.

Tim flew one way.

Grk flew another.

A hundred cones and twenty different flavours of ice cream exploded into the air and came splashing down onto the ground like a shower of multicoloured snow.

The Duke of Macaroni's guards applied the brakes and came to a halt by the entrance to the Colosseum. For the first time they could see who they had been chasing.

Not a terrorist, an assassin or a thief, but a kid.

A kid who was now surrounded by twenty gladiators.

The Duke of Macaroni's men communicated quickly among themselves then turned their bikes round and drove away. They knew what their boss hated more than anything in the world.

Bad publicity.

And what could have been worse publicity than his guards appearing on the front pages of tomorrow's papers, trying to snatch a boy from a bunch of men in skirts?

When Tim opened his eyes he saw a gladiator staring down at him.

The gladiator was wearing a chunky silver helmet, golden armour and a long red cloak. He looked like an extra from a movie.

Sitting up and looking about, Tim saw that he was surrounded by gladiators. There must have been twenty of them, carrying a variety of weapons. Some had spears, others had swords, and one was carrying a net in which to trap his enemies.

For a moment Tim thought he must be going mad. Then he realised what had happened. He must have knocked his head when he fell off the moped and now he was dreaming. In a minute he'd open his eyes and find himself in hospital. His mum and dad would be standing at the end of the bed, looking at him with worried expressions, wondering when he was going to wake up.

One of the gladiators was talking to him in Italian.

'You don't have to talk to me,' said Tim. 'I know you're only a dream.'

'You speak English?' asked the gladiator with a strong accent.

'Yes. Do you?'

'A little,' said the gladiator. 'You are fine? Your bones is broken?'

'I don't think so,' Tim told him.

'Here, stand up.' The gladiator offered an arm.

Tim took it and stood. Behind the gladiators he could see several tourists taking photos. He wondered what they were doing in his dream. Then he began to wonder if he wasn't actually dreaming. This all felt quite real. Perhaps he was awake. But if so, who were these gladiators?

'What are you doing here?' asked another of the gladiators.

'I could ask you the same question,' said Tim.

'Excuse me?'

'I'd like to know what *you're* doing here.'

171

'I work here,' said the gladiator. 'If you pay me five euros you can have one photograph with you, me and the Colosseum.'

Another of the gladiators picked up Tim's moped. He turned the key in the ignition and revved the throttle, but the engine wouldn't start.

'It's not good, my friend,' said the gladiator. 'You will need to call the garage, I think.'

'Where would I find a phone?' asked Tim.

'You want to use mine?'

'If you've got one.'

'No problem.' The gladiator reached into his armour and pulled out a mobile phone. 'You need a number? Or you know a garage already?'

'I've got a number already,' said Tim. He took the phone. 'Thank you. I'll be very quick.'

'Take your time, no problem.' The gladiator smiled, glad of a reason to take a break from shaking his spear and having his picture taken with tourists.

Tim dialled the number scrawled on his sleeve.

The phone rang three times. Then a voice answered. '*Pronto.*'

Tim had been expecting to talk to Alessandra. This was her phone number, after all, so he would have thought she'd answer it. But the voice wasn't hers; it was her father's. Tim said, 'Could I speak to Alessandra, please?'

'Who is this?'

'It's Tim. I've got to speak to Alessandra, please.'

'*Tim*? Who is Tim?'

'The boy from yesterday, at TuttoFood. You helped me. You gave me some money for a taxi. Now I need to speak to Alessandra. It's very important. Can I talk to her, please?'

'I don't think so, Tim.'

'You don't think so? Why not?'

'Because you are not a good friend for my daughter. I am sorry. Now I will say goodbye, Tim.'

'Wait! Please, wait! Just listen to me for one second.'

There was a pause. Then Alessandra's father said, 'Very well. One second. What do you want to say?'

'Have you heard of Massimo Mascarpone?'

'You mean the one who died? The brother of *il Duca*?'

'That's exactly who I mean,' said Tim. 'But he's not dead.'

'Not dead? Not dead? How do you know?'

'I'll tell you,' Tim promised. 'But only if you'll let me speak to Alessandra first.'

Chapter Thirty-Eight

At ten o'clock that morning a taxi pulled up outside the church of Santa Maria dei Gemelli. The doors opened. A man, a boy, a girl and a dog got out. They took two heavy bags from the back of the taxi, paid the driver and walked into the church.

They had just come from the best sports shop in Rome, where they had told the assistant that they were going on a potholing holiday, visiting caves in the mountains. He had supplied them with ropes and harnesses. With these, he'd promised, they could clamber down the trickiest caves in the country.

A bald priest was walking up the aisle of the cool, dark church. He nodded to them. They nodded and smiled back.

The priest glanced at their bags but didn't ask any questions. There's no law against carrying bags into a church.

Once the priest had gone Tim, Alessandra and Salvatore Pecorino hurried down to the end of the church and found a wooden door. It was bolted and secured with a padlock.

Salvatore glanced around, checking that they weren't being watched, then opened his bag and took out a crowbar.

He snapped the padlock from the door and swung it open.

They walked down twenty stone steps and found themselves in a small, dark basement. In one corner there was an altar. In another there were several tombs. In the centre of the basement there was a hole in the floor, surrounded by metal railings.

Tim called through the hole: 'Massimo?'

A distant voice echoed back up: '*Hello-oh-ooh-oooh-ooooh*!'

'Stand back,' ordered Tim. 'We're going to get you out of there.'

Salvatore opened the biggest bag and took out a harness.

Alessandra removed a rope from the other bag.

Salvatore attached the harness to one end of the rope, then looped the other end around the railings and tied it with a secure knot.

He lowered the harness into the hole, giving out more and more of the rope until he felt an answering tug. A couple of minutes later Massimo shouted up, saying he was ready.

Salvatore stepped back and, using all his strength, pulled the rope up. Tim and Alessandra helped him. Even Grk gave a few encouraging yelps.

They hauled and heaved and, millimetre by millimetre, dragged Massimo Mascarpone out of his dungeon and into the crypt of Santa Maria dei Gemelli.

Massimo blinked and stared around the crypt, looking at the altar and the walls as if he had never seen anything so extraordinary.

He had been stuck in the catacombs for many years.

He had grown old. His limbs were tired, his hair was long, his teeth were crooked, his eyes were exhausted and his brain was befuddled. But now, finally, he was out of his prison. With a wild smile, he turned to Tim and grabbed him in a big embrace. '*Grazie!*' he cried. 'Thank you, Tim! Thank you a thousand times!' Then he turned to the others. 'Thank you, thank you, the friends of Tim.'

'*Siamo Italiani*,' said Salvatore. Which means: 'we are Italian'.

Massimo's smile grew even wider as he chatted to Salvatore and Alessandra in their own language, thanking them for rescuing him.

'Er, excuse me?' Tim broke in, not wanting to be rude, but knowing that they couldn't just stand here chatting. 'Hello?'

Massimo turned to him. 'Yes, my friend?'

'I don't want to interrupt, but we should get going. We don't have much time. We mustn't be late.'

'Late?' said Massimo. 'What do you mean, "late"? Late for what?'

'For your next appointment.'

'I have just been buried in a catacomb for eighteen years. I don't have no appointments.'

'Yes, you do. And it's an important one, so you really shouldn't be late. Come on, let's go and find a taxi.'

Chapter Thirty-Nine

All around Italy people were waiting for the Duke of Macaroni.

In kitchens and sitting rooms, bars and cafés, Italian men and women were staring at their televisions, eager to hear his plans for their country.

Some of them loved him. Others hated him.

Some of them trusted him. Others didn't believe a word that came out of his mouth.

Some of them were sure that he was the only person who could save their country. Others thought that they might have to emigrate if *il Duca* became prime minister.

Whoever they were, and whatever they thought of him, all of them wanted to know what he was going to say.

They stared at their TV screens, waiting for the duke to appear.

The duke looked at his reflection in the mirror and smiled. He was feeling confident. He had practised his speech again and again, making every word count. Now he wanted to stand up before the people of Italy and ask them to vote for him.

A make-up girl dabbed his nose with powder. Another combed his hair. They were making him look perfect for the cameras. He took no notice of them, but turned to his advisers and asked, 'How are the figures?'

'Looking good,' said one of his advisers. 'We're expecting at least thirty-five million viewers. Maybe even forty.'

'We should probably go upstairs,' said another adviser. 'If you're ready.'

'Of course I'm ready,' said the duke. 'I've never felt readier in my life.'

The make-up girls stepped aside. The duke eased himself out of his chair and took one final look at his reflection in the mirror.

A handsome man stared back at him.

A handsome man who, he was sure, would soon be the Prime Minister of Italy.

He nodded to his advisers and said, 'Let's go. I don't want to keep forty million people waiting.'

'Good morning,' said the Duke of Macaroni. He had just arrived at the side entrance of the TV studios. Now he was smiling at the security guards. 'I've come to give a speech. Could you let me in, please?'

For a moment neither of the guards replied. They were too surprised. What was the duke doing here? His speech was due to start in three minutes. Why wasn't he upstairs already? Why had he brought Peppi with him, but not his wife, his advisers, or his bodyguards? And who were these three people – this man, this girl and this boy – who were accompanying him instead?

The guards didn't ask any of these questions. Of course they didn't. They were just security guards and he was the Duke of Macaroni. Instead they opened the door and ushered him inside.

One of them hurried up the stairs with him, showing him the way to the studios.

The other picked up his phone and called his boss, the Head of Security. 'Good morning, sir. The Duke of Macaroni has just arrived.'

'I know,' said the Head of Security.

'Do you?'

'Of course I do. I've just seen him. Now, don't bother me, I'm very busy.'

The guard was about to ask how the Head of Security could possibly have seen the duke, since he had only just walked through the door, when the phone went dead.

The guard shrugged his shoulders. If the Head of Security didn't want to talk to him, he didn't mind. He sat back in his chair and turned up the TV. Like everyone else in the country, he couldn't wait to hear what *il Duca* was going to say.

As the Duke of Macaroni swept through the corridors people stared curiously at him and his companions, but they didn't stop him or ask any awkward questions. They stepped aside, allowing him to rush past and get to the studio.

If they had stopped to look a little more carefully they

might have seen that the duke didn't look quite like himself today.

His teeth weren't as white as usual.

His clothes and shoes weren't as expensive as usual.

His face was a little thinner than usual.

And calmer and kinder too.

But he was hurrying so quickly down the corridor that no one had a chance to observe these small details. They simply smiled at him, or waved, or saluted, or wished him 'good luck'.

Earlier this morning no one would have been fooled. When Massimo Mascarpone emerged from the church of Santa Maria dei Gemelli and climbed into the back of a taxi, the driver shifted uncomfortably in his seat and wound down his window. He didn't like carrying tramps in his cab. Particularly tramps who smelt so awful. But the pick-up was outside a church, and a priest was watching, and the driver didn't want to make a fuss in front of a priest, so he took the job, driving the tramp and his friends to a hotel on the other side of town.

Once they were all inside Salvatore's hotel room Massimo took a long, hot shower, using lots of soap, scrubbing years of ingrained dirt from his skin.

When he emerged Salvatore and Alessandra were waiting for him with a razor and a pair of scissors.

They shaved his long beard and cut his even longer hair. Then they dressed him in a black suit, a white shirt and a pair of shiny leather shoes, which might not have looked perfect – they belonged to Salvatore and were much too big for Massimo – but were a great improvement on the dirt-sodden rags which had been his clothes for the past eighteen years.

The lights dimmed. The cameras switched on. The audience went quiet. The Duke of Macaroni walked onto the stage.

He approached the microphone.

The cameras focused on his face.

He looked a little different today.

His teeth weren't as gleamingly white as usual.

His clothes didn't fit so perfectly.

And his expression was different too. He didn't look as confident as normal. Or as arrogant.

He stopped at the microphone and looked around the hallway. Then he gave a shy smile and said, '*Buongiorno.*'

Giovanni Mascarpone, the thirteenth Duke of Macaroni, couldn't believe his eyes.

He had seen a screen showing what was happening on stage. Someone had walked out there, dressed as him.

Was it a joke?

Who would do that? Who would dare?

Shrugging aside his advisers and his bodyguards he pounded down the corridor. Behind him, he could hear shouts. People were telling him to stop. 'Wait,' they were saying. 'Let us take care of this. We'll find out what's going on.' The duke ignored them and charged through the door which led to the stage.

He ran towards the microphone. The place that he was supposed to be standing, giving his speech to the nation.

But before he got there, he stopped.

And stared.

A man was standing at the microphone. Exactly where *he* was supposed to be standing.

And the man was him.

He couldn't be. Of course he couldn't. If that man was him, then he couldn't be himself, and he was.

So who was he?

For a long moment the twins stared at one another.

The Duke of Macaroni looked at the Duke of Macaroni.

Massimo looked at Giovanni.

Giovanni looked at Massimo.

The audience watched them too. So did forty million people, all around Italy, staring at their TV screens.

No one spoke.

No one moved.

Until Giovanni noticed a small dog standing by his brother's side.

Not just any dog.

That dog.

The one who looked like Peppi.

Suddenly everything made sense. He couldn't imagine how the dog had done it, but somehow this horrible mutt had discovered his secret and freed his brother from the catacombs.

The duke felt a surge of fury bubbling through his blood. These dogs! These terrible dogs! Those miserable, horrible, identical dogs. Between them, they had ruined his life.

'I'll kill you!' he whispered.

The cameras were trained on his face, broadcasting his image around the entire country, capturing every sound that he made, even the slightest whisper. But he had forgotten all about them. He'd forgotten the audience. He'd forgotten his speech. He'd forgotten everything, in fact, apart from the little dog who was standing before him.

'I killed Peppi,' he said. 'Now I'm going to kill you too.'

A mad grin spread across his face. And he ran at the dog.

Grk stood frozen to the spot.

So did Massimo.

No one else in the hall moved, either. The journalists, the cameramen, the audience – all of them stared in astonishment at the Duke of Macaroni as he ran across the stage, swung his right leg back and aimed a brutal kick at a little dog.

Just before the duke's shiny, pointed black shoe connected with Grk's head he was knocked sideways by a fist.

He stumbled backwards, clutching his jaw. He swayed for a moment, blinking, as if he were trying to remember something rather important. Where he was, perhaps. Or what he was supposed to be doing here.

And then, as though the whole thing was just too much for him, he closed his eyes and crumpled to the floor.

Massimo Mascarpone, the thirteenth Duke of Macaroni, rubbed his bruised fingers and looked down at his brother. 'I've been wanting to do that for a long time,' he said with a sad smile.

Chapter Forty

Salvatore opened the heavy door of the oven. He reached inside and yanked out a tray of pizza.

'*Ecco*,' he said. '*La pizza della mia famiglia.*'

'The pizza of our family,' Alessandra translated for anyone in the room who couldn't speak Italian.

The large, crisp pizza was covered in tomato, salami and melted mozzarella made from the milk of Salvatore's buffalos.

Using a long, sharp knife, Salvatore cut the pizza into slices, which Alessandra handed around to Tim, Max, Natascha, Mr Malt, Mrs Malt and Massimo Mascarpone, the thirteenth Duke of Macaroni. Then she picked up another piece and said, 'I have forgotten someone, I think.'

'Me,' said her father.

'No, no, not you,' said Alessandra.

'How about yourself?' asked Tim.

'Yes, I will have a piece in one minute. But first I have forgotten someone else. The smallest of us all. Gruk! Gruk! You want some pizza?'

Grk didn't need to be asked twice. He darted across the room, his tail wagging, and crouched excitedly at Alessandra's feet.

She knelt down and fed him the pizza.

Grk ate it fast, licked his lips and begged for another piece.

But he wasn't going to get it. Not yet, anyway. Because right now Massimo was tapping his glass, calling for everyone's attention.

'I would like to make a toast,' announced the Duke of Macaroni. 'I have lost a brother but gained a friend. I would like to propose a toast to Tim, my new friend, and the person who saved my life.' He raised his glass. 'To Tim.'

'*To Tim,*' echoed everyone else in the room, and they all drank a toast to him.

Mr Malt, Mrs Malt, Salvatore and Massimo were drinking the finest bottle of prosecco that could be found in the cellars of the Palazzo Macaroni. Tim, Max, Natascha and Alessandra were drinking orange juice freshly squeezed from fruit that had been picked from trees on the Macaroni estates. Grk had a bowl of water from the tap, and he was very happy with that.

Earlier that day Massimo had taken possession of the palazzo and the possessions that were rightfully his.

Before doing anything else, he had sent his private jet to London to pick up the very worried Malts and Raffifis, and brought them to Italy. He had invited everyone to stay in the Palazzo Macaroni, and tonight, Salvatore and Alessandra were cooking supper for them all.

Massimo's brother was not in the palazzo.

By the time Giovanni Mascarpone regained consciousness and sat up, rubbing his chin and blinking his eyes, the police had been waiting for him. Pushing aside the crowd of screaming journalists they led him down the stairs and out of the building to a waiting car.

More journalists were waiting there, yelling more questions. Their cameras recorded everything, broadcasting these amazing scenes to forty million stunned Italians. Even if any of them still wanted to vote for *il Duca* as their prime minister, he wouldn't be standing in any elections for a long time. He was going to be spending the next few years in a prison cell.

As soon as the duchess discovered what had actually happened to Peppi she started proceedings for divorce. Carla didn't want to spend another minute married to the man who had murdered her dog. Once her divorce was completed, she announced, she would be giving up all political duties and devoting her time and her fortune to a joint venture with the famous vet, Dottore Marcello Ricotta. Together they would build a brand-new animal sanctuary in the centre of the city, *il rifugio di Roma di cane feriti e abbandonati*, the Roman Refuge for Injured and Abandoned Dogs.

As for Alberto and Antonio, they were last seen boarding a plane bound for Rio de Janiero.

When Tim saw that Massimo wasn't going to say anything else, he also tapped his glass.

Everyone turned to look at him.

'I want to say thank you to someone too,' Tim declared. 'She saved me when I was stuck. She showed me where to go and what to do. If you hadn't helped me,

Alessandra, I'd still be searching for Grk on my own.'

'And I'd still be in the catacombs,' said Massimo.

'And your brother would be our prime minster,' added Salvatore.

Tim raised his glass in her direction. '*Grazie mille,* Alessandra. Thank you for everything.'

Alessandra grinned. 'No problem,' she said. 'It was a pleasure for meeting you.' She knelt down and tickled Grk's ears. '*Anche tu, mio piccolo amico.*'

Which means: 'you too, my little friend'.

Grk wagged his tail and licked Alessandra's hand, hoping for another piece of that delicious pizza.